SHOOT FIRST...

As they rode forward, Remington took in as much as he could. The large, elegant ranch house sprawled all over the place.

The four cowhands stood a few feet apart, hands hovering over holstered pistols. Remington could feel the tension build as he and his men rode close to the house.

The front door opened and Peter Van Hook stepped onto the porch.

"I'm Ned Remington, United States Chief Territorial Marshal," Remington said. "I have a warrant for your arrest."

"Open fire, men," Van Hook told his cow hands. "Shoot to kill!"

REMINGTON #7

RED RIVER REVENGE

JAMES CALDER BOONE

AVON BOOKS ◆ NEW YORK

REMINGTON #7: RED RIVER REVENGE is an original publication of
Avon Books. This work has never before appeared in book form.

AVON BOOKS
A division of
The Hearst Corporation
105 Madison Avenue
New York, New York 10016

Copyright © 1988 by James Calder Boone
Published by arrangement with the author
Produced in cooperation with Taneycomo Productions, Inc.,
Branson, Missouri
Library of Congress Catalog Card Number: 87-91445
ISBN: 0-380-75559-9

First Avon Books Printing: May 1988

AVON TRADEMARK REG. U.S. PAT. OFF. AND IN OTHER COUNTRIES, MARCA
REGISTRADA, HECHO EN U.S.A.

Printed in the U.S.A.

K–R   10   9   8   7   6   5   4   3   2   1

Chapter One

Ned Remington leaned over and kissed his daughter on the forehead and wondered if she even knew he was there in the room with her.

Katy didn't respond except to shift her eyes for a brief instant to glance up at the tall, lanky man who stood beside her rocking chair. There was no expression in her dark, deep-set eyes, no sign that she recognized her father. She blinked once, then went back to staring out the window of her small room in the convent. With a vacant expression in her eyes, she gazed out at the courtyard garden, as she had done ever since her father arrived an hour earlier.

A shaft of afternoon sunlight streamed through the sparkling clean window from a high angle missing Katy's stolid face by a few inches, but bathing her plain yellow dress in a bright golden sheen.

A feeling of profound sadness swept through Ned Remington as he watched his pathetic daughter rocking back and forth, back and forth, in the padded wooden chair, never varying the slow, even pace of her constant motion. It was the same heartsick sense of utter helplessness that always came over him when he visited his mentally ill daughter at the convent.

1

The constant creaking of the rocking chair set his nerves on edge, adding to his feeling of frustration. He took a deep breath, fighting back the emotions that welled up in him, and strolled over to the window.

Three years before, Katy had been a bright, beautiful, vivacious, budding, young lady of eighteen. And then Katy had been brutally raped by a stranger and left for dead. Her mother, Ned's pretty wife Alice, had been viciously raped and tragically murdered at the same time, by the same depraved man who had attacked Katy.

Each time he saw his daughter, he thought she looked more and more like her mother. Katy had dark brown hair and a slender face like his own, but her facial features, the smoothness of her cheeks, the deep brown eyes, the small delicate nose, the sensual fullness of her mouth, all reminded him of his beloved dead wife.

At twenty-one, Katy Remington was still a beautiful young woman, but her mind was gone. If it weren't for her inanimate, zombie-like condition, Ned knew that she would have attracted a dozen beaus by now. In fact, she probably would have been married by now. Just before the double tragedy that changed Katy's life, several nice young lads were beginning to show interest in her. Since the tragedy, nobody could get through to Katy, and the two young fellows who used to visit her at the convent had stopped coming to see her after the first six months.

Each time Ned Remington came to see his daughter, his heart broke a little more with the ache of knowing that she couldn't communicate with him. As he watched her, it was like looking at the pale ghost of the vibrant, cheerful, fun-loving girl she used to be. The way she sat so still in her chair, poised, hands folded in her lap, it was as if she were posing for an artist's portrait. It was as if she were already a painting.

At times, like now, she reminded Ned of one of the graceful, immobile, marble statues that adorned the long corridors and the quiet vestibule of the nunnery. And yet, beneath that impenetrable, protective wall she'd built around herself, she was a living, breathing human being with warm flesh and blood. And somewhere deep down inside her, Ned knew that his Katy had feelings and emotions that were too painful for her to face.

Even though it had been three years since the traumatic attack, Katy had never gotten over the shock of seeing her mother raped and murdered. She had never recovered from the effects of being brutally raped herself by the same cruel, ruthless brute who had viciously attacked her mother while Katy was forced to watch. Katy had retreated into a shell, a world of her own where only she knew what went on in her mind, if anything.

Ned would be forever grateful to the kind and loving sisters at the convent for taking Katy under their protective wings after the tragedy. As Chief United States Deputy Marshal for Judge Samuel Parkhurst Barnstall in Stone County, Missouri, Ned Remington was gone a great deal of the time and it eased his conscience some to know that Katy was in good hands. His job was to track down criminals and bring them back to Galena to face Judge Barnstall's tough interpretation of law and justice. Ned always visited Katy before he left Galena on an assignment and when he returned, he always headed straight for the convent, hopeful that some miracle had brought his daughter out of her deep stupor. He had been gone three weeks this time and had just returned that afternoon.

The friendly nuns gave Katy the tender loving care she needed in his absence. They kept her clean, her hair brushed to a sheen and usually curled, and they dressed her in pretty frocks they sewed themselves. Although Katy's progress was painfully slow and often discouraging, Ned was grateful to the nuns for their continuous efforts on Katy's behalf. As a result of their loving care, Katy had rallied for a brief time before she withdrew back into her shell. She had uttered only two words to him since that time. The same word, on two separate occasions. "Love." He had nearly exploded with anguished joy when she had spoken the word. It hadn't been much, one word each time, but to him, it had been a miracle that she had even spoken. It had been enough to give him hope that someday she would recover completely.

He glanced over at Katy and felt the all too familiar pain stab at his heart. It just tore him apart to see her rocking back and forth that way, staring out the window, her mind like that of a demented child.

Katy didn't even have the mind of a child, he thought bitterly as he studied his daughter's expressionless face. A child could laugh and cry, and sing and play, and smile and talk. Katy couldn't do any of these things. She just sat in that damned rocking chair and stared out the window day after day as life passed her by.

Ned Remington sighed deeply and glanced out the window, as if by doing so, he could somehow share

her thoughts. He wondered if Katy could see the pro-
fusion of colorful flowers in the neatly manicured
courtyard garden, or the black-robed nuns who
tended the garden. He wondered if she saw the birds
that lived in the sanctuary as they flitted from the tree
branches to the birdbath and back to the trees again.
She seemed to be mesmerized by the bubbling fountain in the peaceful garden pool, but he doubted that
she knew or understood what she was looking at.

"Goodbye, Katy. I'll be back," he said in a gentle
voice, wishing with all of his heart that she could
understand him, that she could answer him.

Again Katy shifted her eyes to look up at him, but
it was as if she was looking through him, not at him.
The rocking chair creaked to a stop and Katy sat perfectly still. As she gazed up at her father, her dark
eyes were dull and lifeless, glazed over as a dead
person's eyes would be.

Suddenly panic-stricken, Ned's breath caught in
his throat as he stared down at his motionless daughter for a long moment. His heart skipped a beat. His
stomach fluttered with a foreboding apprehension. He
had to force himself to tear his eyes away from hers
long enough to watch the front of her bright yellow
dress. When he saw the delicate fabric rise and fall
with her slow, steady breathing, his hands broke out
in a cold sweat. Katy was still alive.

"I love you, Katy," he said with a sigh of relief. He
reached down and tenderly brushed a loose strand of
hair away from her face.

Katy continued to stare at him, a blank expression
on her face. Suddenly her mouth quivered and con-
torted, as if she were struggling to form a word. And
then, for the first time ever since the tragedy, Katy

Remington seemed to look directly at her father.

"L-l-love . . . you," she stammered, her voice so low, he could barely hear her.

Remington's heart soared with the joy he felt at his daughter's words. He didn't know if she knew what she was saying, or whether she was just mimicking his own words. He didn't care. She had spoken and it restored his faith that someday Katy would come out of her shell and become a normal, happy girl again.

"Oh, my little Katy, I love you so much," he beamed. Without thinking, he reached out with his long arms and quickly leaned down to take her in his arms so he could hold her tight.

The abrupt movement toward her triggered something deep inside Katy. She quickly drew back away from him, pressing her head hard against the back of her chair. Ned saw a dark shadow of terror cross over her face. And then there was no expression at all in her dark eyes as Katy once again stared out the window at the bubbling fountain in the courtyard garden. The rocking chair began its slow, ceaseless squeaking as Katy set it to rocking back and forth again.

Ned's heart sank to his stomach like a lead ball. He cursed under his breath, realizing that he shouldn't have made a sudden move toward his daughter. He had been so overcome with joy, he just wanted to hold her in his arms, and tell her that everything was going to be all right. Instead, he had frightened her and sent her scampering like a startled lizard back into the safety of her mindless world.

He stayed with her a few more minutes, the monotonous creaking of the rocking chair a constant reminder of Katy's delicate condition. Finally, he could no longer bear to watch her.

Heartsick, Remington retrieved his black Stetson from a table near the door. Without another word, he walked out of Katy's room, hat in hand. His boots rang hollow on the highly polished floor of the long corridor as he made his way toward the front entrance gate. As he walked through the hushed vestibule with its many religious statues and paintings, he nodded and smiled at a pair of elderly nuns at the far end of the large, quiet room. The nuns, wearing black habits and silver rosaries, nodded back. Ned glanced at one of the graceful marble statues near the front door of the convent and suddenly resented it because it reminded him of his daughter.

Remington squinted when he stepped outside into the bright sunlight. He slid his black Stetson onto his head, tugged the brim down to shade his eyes from the late afternoon sun as he walked along the flower-lined path that led from the front door of the nunnery to the entrance gate of the tall stone wall that surrounded the grounds of the convent. The big, heavy wooden gate whined on rusty hinges when he pushed it open. He closed it behind him and headed for the hitchrail where he had left his horse, a big Missouri trotter named Neal.

Once he was beyond the stone wall that surrounded the convent, Ned felt the tension creep back into his shoulder muscles, the tautness that came from the anger he'd suppressed while he was inside the sanctuary of the nunnery. When he reached over to untie his horse from the hitchrail, he realized that both of his hands were clenched to hard fists. His hatred for the stranger who had raped his daughter and killed his wife intensified every time he saw Katy.

Shortly after the tragedy, Remington had learned

the stranger's identity. Lucas Passmore. An elusive no-account, a fugitive with no place to call home. A drifter who shied away from towns and who left very little sign that he even existed. A ghost of a man who seemed to disappear like a wisp of smoke whenever Remington was hot on his trail. A cruel loner who apparently had no friends and only an occasional riding companion. A degenerate bastard who had raped and murdered more than once.

According to a neighbor who had seen the stranger leave Remington's ranch, Passmore was a short, stocky man, sandy-haired, who wore filthy, rumpled clothes, a battered hat and boots that looked like they'd never seen the backside of a shining cloth. The neighbor, Hank Bushmeyer, hadn't known about the attack on the Remington women when he passed the stranger on the road. But Bushmeyer had gotten a good look at the man who rode away from the Remington ranch and later told Ned that the stranger was real mean-looking and that there was something odd about the man's eyes. After further investigation, Remington had learned that one of Passmore's eyelids had been slashed and sewn back together so that the eyelid was half-closed all the time.

Ned Remington had vowed to bring the murdering rapist to justice and he never stopped looking for him. When he wasn't busy with assignments from Judge Barnstall, Ned spent many hours in the saddle tracking Lucas Passmore, following leads. He had almost caught Passmore once, but the slit-eyed bastard had outwitted him.

Remington could wait. He knew for certain that someday Passmore would pay for his heinous crimes.

These were the thoughts that Remington couldn't shake as he rode the short mile back to Galena. Since he had just come back from a three-week assignment, he hoped he'd have some free time to go looking for Passmore again.

A gentle breeze brushed across his face and played at the back of his neck as Ned rode into town. The day had been hot and sticky and the coolness of the late afternoon seemed to have drawn the townspeople to the main street like flies to honey. Carriages and horses clogged the dusty street. Long-skirted women strolled along the boardwalk and men who were finished with their work for the day began to gather at the saloons. The stone courthouse where Judge Barnstall held court sat in the middle of the town square and nearby were the hard wooden benches where several elderly gentlemen had gathered to chat while they whittled on chunks of wood with dull knives.

As Ned reined his horse up near the town square and got a whiff of the heady aroma of steaming spiced beef that drifted over from Bessie's Restaurant, he suddenly realized how hungry he was. He hadn't bothered to eat lunch that day. Instead, he had headed straight for the convent after he'd delivered his prisoners to the guards earlier that afternoon and now his stomach was beginning to growl. He ran his fingers over the rough stubble of whiskers on his chin and decided to go ahead and eat an early supper.

He dismounted, looped the reins over the hitchrail and adjusted his gunbelt before he cut across a corner of the town square to get to Bessie's. Twin leather holsters hung from the gunbelt. A .44 caliber converted Remington New Model Army fit snug in one holster and the other held a Colt .44. When he had arrived in Galena earlier that afternoon, he had put his other weapons in his room, the Smith & Wesson .38 that hung from the saddlehorn and his rifle, a '73 Winchester, .44-40 caliber.

Ned was six feet tall, lean, square-jawed. He took long, easy strides and looked as graceful as a proud buck as he walked. He crossed the hard, dirt street to the restaurant and had just opened the door when he saw Frank Shaw, one of the other deputies, heading his way. He paused and waited, his hand still wrapped around the brass door knob.

"The judge wants to see you, Ned," Frank Shaw said when he got closer. Shaw had at least a dozen years on Remington. With his gray hair and stooped shoulders, he looked old and tired, but Shaw was ex-tremely strong and could hold his own with any of the other deputies.

"Now?" Remington asked as he drank in the smell of food. "Can it wait until after supper?"

"I think it'd better be now, Ned," Frank said. "Judge Barnstall's been asking for you."

"What does he want?" Ned asked. He pushed the restaurant door closed and dropped his hand away from the brass knob.

"I don't know, but judging from the papers his clerk delivered to him while I was there, I'd say Barnstall's going to send you out on another case right away."

"Were they warrants?" Ned asked.

"I couldn't be sure, but they looked like it," Shaw said.

"But I just got back from eating trail dust for three

hot, stinkin' weeks," Remington protested. "I need some time off."

"Tell it to the judge," Shaw smiled, a twinkle in his old blue eyes.

Chapter Two

Ned Remington climbed the steps that led to the second story of the old stone courthouse. He wore no coat on this hot day and his shiny deputy's badge was pinned to the front of his shirt. He paused in front of Judge Barnstall's office door and brushed a smudge of trail dust from his trousers before he knocked on the door.

"Come in, Ned," came the loud, booming voice from behind the closed door.

Remington opened the door and stepped inside the familiar room that smelled of wood and leather and the fine Virginia tobacco of the cigars Judge Barnstall kept in the mahogany cigar box on his desk.

"How'd you know it was me?" he asked, a smile playing on his lips. He closed the door behind him and walked across the room.

Judge Barnstall glanced up from the sheaf of papers on his cherrywood desk.. He was a stocky man, broadshouldered, thick chested. When he stood, he was not quite five foot eleven, but when he sat on his high wooden bench in the courtroom, he appeared tall enough to tower over anyone else in the room. He wore a dark suit, a white shirt with the top button unbuttoned, his thin silk tie untied but held in place by the collar of his shirt. His black robe hung on the clothes tree in the corner of the room. In another corner of the room stood a mahogany liquor cabinet and next to that, a large globe of the world perched on top of a walnut stand.

Barnstall kept his office neat and orderly, which made the room seem larger than it actually was. The bookshelves behind his desk held his matched set of leather-bound, gold-embossed lawbooks and at least as many odd-sized, dogeared books on the history of the land. The judge referred to the books often, as he did to the two large parchment maps that adorned the wall near the globe. One map showed the fine details of the southwestern United States, and the other map was of the Indian Nations. The judge's framed law degree from Harvard University hung in the middle of another wall, near the Seth Thomas clock.

"Simple logic and deduction," Barnstall said in his loud, clear voice. He leaned back in his oversized leather chair and looked up at Remington with piercing blue eyes. "You always knock three times, Ned. Everyone else knocks four times."

"I didn't realize that," Remington said. He scratched his chin and thought about it.

"If you plan to become a good deputy someday, you should learn to be more observant, Ned."

Remington sensed the teasing reprimand in Barnstall's stern voice. Without feeling smug about it, Ned knew that he was the best deputy sheriff around. Judge Barnstall knew it, too. That's why he gave Ned the most difficult assignments.

"Yes, your honor," Ned said without cracking a smile. "I'll take your advice."

"Sit down, will you?" the judge said in a grumpy voice. "You're too damned tall and I'm getting a crick in my neck lookin' up at you."

"Yes, sir." Ned grinned at the older man and tapped the brim of his hat in a salute. As he settled down into the comfortable leather-padded chair facing Barnstall, Ned saw that the judge's desk was more cluttered than usual. Besides the papers that were directly in front of Samuel Barnstall, there were notes scattered across the desk top, all neatly penned on foolscap paper, evidence that the judge had not been idle. A stack of clean foolscap sat off to the side and next to that, a wooden pen rested by the inkwell.

The aromatic cigar box sat on one corner of the desk, nearly hidden from view by the notes that rested on top of it. Remington could see only the corner of the box where the likeness of an elephant had been delicately carved into the fine-grained wood. On the other corner of the cherrywood desk were the two plaques that were familiar to Ned. One of them was inscribed with Barnstall's full name, Judge Samuel Parkhurst Barnstall. The other plaque, the judge's favorite, bore the Latin legend: *Ignorantia legis neminen excusat*. Remington knew that the translation meant: Ignorance of the law is no excuse.

Pushed to the side of the desk were the two stacked box frames that held important papers. The brass bell that Barnstall used occasionally to summon his clerk was tucked out of the way behind one of the plaques.

Judge Barnstall thumbed through the papers in front of him, pulled some of them out of the stack.

"Here are the warrants for two men I want you to bring in," he said as he handed one set of the parchment papers across his desk to Remington. "The top one there is for Paco Gaton, alias *El Cuchillo*."

Ned took the papers and glanced at the top one. *"El Cuchillo*. The Blade," he said with a cold edge to his voice. His brow wrinkled to a frown. "The man must be good with a knife to earn a nickname like that."

"That'd be my guess," Barnstall said wryly.

"I've heard of this Paco Gaton," Remington said as he jabbed a finger at the name on the paper. "From what I remember, he's very quick with a .45 Colt."

"Let's hope you're quicker," Barnstall said as he pulled another paper from his stack. "The second warrant is for one Norville Haskins. You know him?" He glanced over at Remington.

"No. Never heard of him."

The judge nodded for Ned to read the warrants as he looked down at his own copies of the documents. "Both men are wanted for murder and cattle rustling," he said in a clear, crisp voice as he began to read aloud from one of the warrants. "To wit: the wilful shooting and killing of one Woodrow Miller, a rancher, and one Frank Twokill, a Cherokee drover who worked for Miller. And the stealing of a herd of cattle in excess of three hundred head of beeves from the Mirror M Ranch near Osage, Arkansas."

"The Mirror M. That would be Woodrow Miller's ranch, I assume," Remington said as he glanced over at the judge.

"Yes. Take note of the sketch of the brand my clerk has drawn on the next page." Barnstall flipped the page with his stubby fingers and nodded to Remington to do the same.

Remington studied the drawing. "It looks like two diamonds, side by side." He picked up the paper and held it at a distance. "I can see it now. An M with an upsidedown M right under it. The Mirror M."

"That's right. You'll be looking for cattle with that brand as proof of the rustling."

"The brand is so plain, it'd be easy to alter it with a running iron, " Remington commented as he stared down at the drawing and imagined other configurations of the mirrored M.

"And I trust you're smart enough to recognize the original brand when you see it." Barnstall looked over at Ned, a questioning look on his face.

Remington chuckled. He liked Judge Barnstall. The old codger had a dry sense of humor, but he was tough as a boot in the courtroom. Barnstall always gave a man a fair trial, but he also had no qualms about dishing out the harshest of punishments to those who were found guilty. Ned had been a deputy long before Governor Benjamin Gratz Brown had appointed Sam Barnstall judge of Stone County, Missouri, and Ned hadn't liked working under Barnstall's predecessor, Judge Binder. Too many times Ned had brought in criminals who never saw the inside of the courtroom. The prisoners were released without going to trial because of the money that lined Judge Binder's pockets, and Ned got to the point where he thought his own efforts were a waste of time. Sam Barnstall was different. He wanted his territory to be a safe place for decent folks to live and in the short time he'd been judge, Barnstall had earned the reputation of the hanging judge.

Ned glanced up at one of the maps on the wall. "Osage, Arkansas. That's not too far from here. A three-day ride if I push it. I could be back in a week."

"It's not going to be that easy, Ned. You haven't

heard the rest of it. Turn back to the first page." The sound of riffling papers was the only sound in the quiet room. "These two unsavory sonsofbitches," Barnstall said, and then he quoted directly from the warrant, "did then take said herd into the Nations and drive them over into Texas where they did sell said illegally obtained stock to a rancher named Peter Van Hook." He glanced at Ned. "You'll find that bastard's name on a warrant as well, as soon as my clerk finishes the paperwork."

Ned leaned back in the chair and let the papers rest on his leg. "So, you're sending me down into Texas and I'm looking for three men, not two."

"Yes, Ned. You'll have to take provisions to last you at least two or three weeks. Take a couple of the other deputies with you. I'll leave it up to you to decide on which men you want to accompany you."

"The best we've got," Ned sighed. "I'll probably take Jim Early, for one."

"Early's up in Springfield on another case," Barnstall said. "I don't figure he'll be back for a few days and we can't wait on this one."

"Damn," Ned muttered.

"What makes Paco Gaton and Norville Haskins so damned bad is that this isn't the first time they've killed or rustled cattle."

"Cattle rustling is common in this territory," Ned said. "So is murder."

"But, this case is unprecedented on two other counts," said the judge. "One, this is the first time, that we know of, that they've gone into the Nations with contraband. And two, there was an eyewitness to the killing of Woody Miller. She can identify both Gaton and Haskins."

"She?" asked Remington. His brow wrinkled to a puzzled frown.

"Yes," said Judge Barnstall in a matter-of-fact tone. "She's hiding out and you'll have to find her and bring her back, too, once you catch these culprits. We need her to testify in court as to what she saw and heard. She'll be our star witness."

"She?" Remington repeated. He grabbed the loose papers from his knee and sat up straight.

"Yes. Woody's daughter," Barnstall said as he leaned forward. "Woodrow Miller was murdered in cold blood. Shot in the back. His daughter was off picking berries along Osage Creek when it happened. She hid when the shooting started, but she saw the whole bloody thing. Hell, she's the one who swore out a complaint against Paco Gaton and Norville Haskins in the first place. We need her to testify."

"Then, why isn't she right here, right now, to tell us about it?" Remington jabbed his finger at the desk to emphasize his point.

"She's hiding out," the judge said calmly. "She's scared, Ned. She doesn't want to come up here to Missouri and testify in court."

"How'd you get her to swear out a complaint if she's so damned shy?" Remington asked.

"She saw her father killed, Ned. Naturally she wants to see the guilty parties brought to justice for their crimes."

"But not enough to come to Galena to testify against them. Is that what you're saying?" Ned didn't know why he felt so irritable. Maybe it was because his own daughter Katy had seen her mother murdered and Katy had been left so helpless that she couldn't do anything about it if she had the opportunity. And now, Judge Barnstall was telling him about a girl who apparently wouldn't lift a finger to see her father's murderers hang.

"I told you, she's scared, Ned." Judge Barnstall's voice was firm, but no louder than usual. He shifted position and as he sat up straighter in the chair, his thick chest seemed to swell against the fabric of his white shirt. "You're a damned good deputy, Ned, the best I've got, but you can't always pick and choose the circumstances of your assignments. If you don't want to take this job, I'll give it to someone else."

Remington glanced at the warrants again, then tossed them on the edge of the judge's desk and leaned back into the chair. He propped an elbow on each arm of the chair, folded his hands, and let them rest against his chest.

"So, if I understand you right, your honor," he said, "not only am I to round up the two cattle-rustling murderers and the man they sold the illegal beeves to, but I'm also to drag a girl in here who doesn't want to be dragged."

"You understand me right, Chief Deputy Marshal Remington," Barnstall said with a smile. "You want the assignment?"

"You know that I'll be risking my neck if some jittery little pea-brained lawman decides to string me up for kidnapping a young girl against her will, don't you?"

Barnstall laughed, shook his head. "There's a certain amount of risk involved in any of the cases you take on as Chief Deputy Marshal. I think you can certainly handle one fragile young woman, Ned. She'll come with you if you talk to her, if you explain how important her testimony is to this case."

"If I can find her," Ned said with a hint of sarcasm.

"She's hiding out in the Nations," Barnstall said.

"That's a mighty big territory, your honor. Got any idea what she looks like?"

The stocky judge settled back in his chair and began to relax. "The girl's a half-breed," he said. "Her ma was a Cherokee. This Frank Twokill, the Cherokee drover who was killed," he said as he pointed to the name on the warrant, "Twokill was her uncle, on her mother's side. After her father and uncle were killed, the girl got word to us and I had Tom Beck ride down and take her statement. You might want to talk to him."

"That's rather unusual procedure, isn't it, sir?" asked Remington.

Judge Barnstall sat up tall, his broad shoulders thrown back so that again, his chest seemed to puff out against the front of his shirt. His pudgy cheeks flushed crimson as he banged his clenched fist on his desk.

"Ned," he boomed in the loud voice he usually reserved for the courtroom, "I don't give a damn how we get the information, whether it be in Indian sign language or smoke signals. This gal's statement is the best deposition I've ever seen on paper, in or out of a court of law. I signed these warrants on the strength of her testimony and I want these miserable sonsof-bitches brought in and hanged right outside that window over there." His arm shot straight out as he pointed to the window that was covered by a closed curtain.

"I understand, your honor," Remington said. "Is that all, then?"

"That's enough, isn't it?" the judge said as he settled back down after his emotional outburst.

"Yes. Where do I find this Miller girl?"

"She's not just a girl," Barnstall smiled. "She's all of nineteen and eligible. Beck said she's as pretty as a prairie flower and she's educated, too."

"Oh, I see," said Remington. "So you sent Tom down to talk to her and now he's sweet on her. Why in the hell didn't he bring her back?"

"He couldn't talk her into it," Barnstall said. "Besides, I sent Deputy Beck down there to take her statement. I didn't tell him to bring her back up here. Now that I've heard her story, I'm leaving that up to you, Ned."

"If I can find her, I'll bring her back," Ned said, "even if I have to walk every damned step of the way carrying her over my shoulder."

"Now that's the Ned Remington I appointed as my Chief Deputy Sheriff," Barnstall beamed.

"Does the pretty young lady have a name, or am I going into this thing totally blind?" Remington asked.

The judge picked up one of his notes and read from it. "Her Christian name's Lina, Lina Miller, and she's hiding out in a place called Tishomingo."

"Tishomingo? Where in the hell is that?" Remington got up and walked over to the maps on the wall.

"North of the Texas border," the judge said.

Remington glanced at both maps, then traced his finger across the one of the Indian Nations. "Here it is. Tishomingo is just north of the Red River, not too far from the Texas border. That's a far piece from Osage, Arkansas."

"It's a good stretch of the legs," Barnstall agreed.

Remington turned and looked at the judge. "Why

would a nineteen-year-old girl ride that far to hide out? There are dozens of places near Osage where she could have concealed herself."

"According to Tom Beck, the poor child's an orphan." Sam Barnstall glanced down at the notes he'd made on the foolscap. "Lina is staying with another uncle in Tishomingo, a Charlie Killbuck. Her ma passed away when she was twelve and she's pretty bitter about her father's death from what Tom says. She wants scalps."

"And she plans to take the scalps herself?"

"She's stubborn enough to try it, according to Beck."

"An eye for an eye. It's her Indian blood." Remington shook his head. "She'd never stand a chance up against those two hardened bastards."

"I know. And the problem is that Paco Gaton and his partner saw her after the killings. She ran away and hid, but she knows they saw her real good and they're hunting hard for her."

Remington let out a low whistle.

"Anything else I should know?" he sighed.

"I want those three men brought in alive," Barnstall said with determination. "I don't care how badly beaten up they are, I just want to see them stand before my bench and receive the maximum punishment for their crimes."

"O.K. Now, where do I look for Gaton and the other two jaspers?"

"Friends of the Millers tracked the herd to the Red River Station, just over the border."

Remington turned to the map, found Tishomingo again, then traced a path down to the Texas border. "Right smack dab on the Chisholm Trail."

"You might want to look around Fort Worth, too, Ned. My guess is that Van Hook is selling beef down there after altering the brands."

"Probably."

"You break this case and I think that will put a pretty big ring out of business," Barnstall said with a big sigh.

"Ring?"

"It looks that way. We've got rustling complaints from all over Arkansas and Missouri. And I plan to put a stop to it."

Ned Remington strolled over and picked up the warrants from the desk, folded them in half. "It looks like I've got my work cut out for me."

There was a light tapping on the door.

"Come in, Lucius," Judge Barnstall said without hesitation.

The door opened and Lucius Robson, a lean, young man in his late teens, entered the room. He carried a few loose papers in his hand. "Here's the warrant for Peter Van Hook," the clerk said as he walked across the small room and delivered the documents to Barnstall.

"Thank you, Lucius," the judge said. "That's all for now. You can go home now."

A grin spread across Robson's face. He nodded, then turned and walked out of the room, closed the door behind him.

Barnstall glanced over the documents, handed one copy of the warrant to Remington, kept the other for himself. "That's all you need."

"I'll leave before dawn tomorrow," Remington said. "I'll get some miles behind me before it gets too damned hot out there."

"Good idea. Who're you going to take with you?"

"I'll take Tom Beck with me since he's familiar with the case. Frank Shaw, too, if he'll come."

"The court will cover their expenses," the judge said. And then he looked up at Ned with those piercing blue eyes. "Good luck and God speed."

Chapter Three

Ned Remington came up over the small rise and hauled back on the reins when he saw the sparsely-settled valley that stretched out ahead of him. The Missouri trotter stopped short, its black, sweat-sleeked hide glistening in the sunlight. The horse cocked its ears and waited patiently as the deputy marshal scanned the land.

Ned had expected the town of Tishomingo to be bigger, more populated. He had expected to see dozens of tipis clustered around a communal fire pit, and Indian ponies huddled together in a pole corral. Instead, small, earth-colored, adobe huts dotted the land. Not more than twenty huts, he thought, all widely scattered. And all across the valley, small flocks of sheep grazed in lush, green pastures. He could see some people moving about, but from that distance they looked like little brown ants. Field workers, horsemen who seemed in no hurry, and the shepherds who tended their flocks.

Way off to his left, the Red River shimmered in the afternoon sunlight like a diamond ribbon as it wound its way through thick stands of trees. The buildings that were clustered near the river were partially hidden from view by the trees.

"Not much of a town, is it?" Remington said to the other two deputies as they rode up beside him and tugged on their reins. The trio of lawmen had been on the hot, dusty trail for a week now and the horses were beginning to show their weariness. All three animals carried heavy saddlebags.

"Tishomingo is only a small, peaceful, Indian village," Tom Beck said. "That's why Lina Miller wanted to come down here and hide out at her uncle's place. She has enough Cherokee blood in her to blend in with the others of the village."

Tom Beck, like the half-breed girl they were looking for, was half Cherokee, on his mother's side. His father was Scotch-Irish, but he had inherited the black hair and dark brown eyes of his mother's heritage. Tom was twenty-eight, five years younger than Remington. At five foot seven, he was also five inches shorter than his friend. When he was young, his parents had lived with his mother's tribe and because he had learned much from his wise Cherokee grandfather, Beck was the best tracker Remington had ever met.

"Is that the Red River over there?" Frank Shaw asked as he pointed off to the left. He tugged his sweat-stained hat down far enough for the wide brim to shield his sensitive blue eyes from the overhead sun. Although he was older than the other two men, he showed no sign of tiring from the long trip.

"Yes," said Beck. "You can just barely see the riverfront buildings where the white men live. That's a busy little harbor with all the ships that come and go. At least it was when I rode through here a year ago."

"How do the whites and the Indians get along?" Remington asked.

"They don't mix with each other except to do business," Beck said.

"What business?" Shaw asked, still staring off toward the glistening river.

"The white fellows buy wool and meat from the Cherokees and ship it downstream, where it's sold for a profit. In turn, the Indians buy trade goods and supplies from the riverfront merchants. They get along."

Remington felt the hot sun on his back where it burned through the dark fabric of his heavy green shirt. His buckskin jacket rode atop his bedroll behind the saddle, held in place by leather thongs, and he was tempted to remove his shirt and stuff it back there, too. He tugged at the damp kerchief around his neck and felt little relief from the air that cooled only the small portion of his neck that was exposed.

"Now, Judge Barnstall said that friends of the Millers had tracked the herd of stolen cattle to the Red River Station," he said. "That must be right across the river, then."

"Well, actually, it was Lina Miller's uncle, Charlie Killbuck, who tracked the cattle," Beck said. "That's what Lina told me. Charlie Killbuck is the one she's supposed to be staying with here. She was planning to leave the day after I talked to her in Osage, Arkansas, to come down here."

"Then we're not really sure she's here in Tishomingo," Remington said, thinking aloud.

"Oh, she's here," Beck laughed. "That gal's got spunk and if she says she's gonna do something, she's gonna do it. And nobody's going to get in her way."

"Barnstall said she was determined," Ned said with a smile.

"Stubborn as a jackass would be a better way to put it." Beck shook his head. "I tried my damndest to get her to go back to Galena with me so she'd have some protection, but she'd have no part of it. She said she wouldn't quit until she held the bloody scalps of those murdering bastards in her hands. Those were her words, not mine."

"Well, I promised Barnstall I'd bring her back to testify, even if I had to carry her on my shoulders," Ned said.

"It may take all three of us to tote her back there," Beck said.

Remington smiled again and wiped the sweat from his brow. "So the Red River Station is just across the river from here."

"No. No, it isn't," Tom Beck said.

"But I thought . . ."

"No," said Beck again. "This is just the upper part of the Red. The Station is across the main body of the Red, way south of here, just across the border of Texas. We'll cross the river here and then there's a good stretch of land to cover before we get to the main part of the Red where we'll have to cross it again. A day's ride, at least. Maybe two."

"Damn," Remington said. "Well, that's what we'll have to do, then. We've got to find those rustled cattle if we can. The judge needs the evidence to nail this case down tight."

"Well, it's for sure those beeves still exist out there somewhere," Shaw said.

"What do you mean, Frank?" A puzzled look came

over Remington's face as he looked over at the older deputy.

"I mean the thieves wouldn't be dumb enough to slaughter three hundred head of cattle in this kind of weather," Shaw said as he flapped his open shirt collar back and forth. "The meat would rot before they could sell it all. No, those bastards'll peddle the cattle on the hoof."

"I know. Well, let's find the girl and get out of here." Remington pulled himself up tall in the saddle, adjusted his hat. He looked out across the peaceful valley and then glanced at Tom Beck. "You got any idea where this Charlie Killbuck lives?"

Beck's horse became restless and took a couple of sidesteps. Beck tightened the reins and reached over and patted the strawberry roan on the neck. "Hold on, Captain," he said. "No, I don't know where he lives. Lina told me that he raises sheep here in Tishomingo. That's all I know."

"Hell, everybody raises sheep in Tishomingo, from what I see," Ned said.

"Killbuck won't be hard to find," Tom said with a grin. "The people are friendly here. Someone will point us in the right direction."

Remington snapped the reins, pulled them to the right and followed the wagon-rutted road that cut through the Indian village. The other two deputies rode right behind him. The trio stopped at the first adobe hut they came to.

The elderly Cherokee man in front of the adobe stood perfectly still, as he had done for several minutes as he watched the deputies ride up. He leaned against the long stick in his hand, using it for support. The flesh of his wrinkled, bronzed chest and arms looked as tough as tanned leather. He wore a breech-clout, and around his neck, colorful beads.

"Hello," Remington said to the man. He tipped his hat. "Do you speak English?"

The old man nodded once.

"We're looking for Charlie Killbuck. Can you tell us where he lives?" Ned asked politely.

The Indian looked over each man in turn, then stared at the shiny marshal's badge that Remington wore on his shirt.

"No," he said. His voice was low and feeble and sounded like he had a dozen pebbles lodged in his throat.

Remington was surprised by the old man's answer. Figuring that the Indian didn't understand him, he tried again, speaking slowly and distinctly. "Charlie Killbuck. A Cherokee like you. Lives here in Tisho-mingo. Where is his adobe?"

The old man shook his head, his lips pinched together.

Remington turned to Tom Beck. "I don't think he understands me," he said. "Can you talk to him?"

Beck moved his horse closer to the man and spoke Cherokee words that Ned didn't understand.

The old Indian listened, then turned and stared up at Remington with eyes that were as cold and hard as two nuggets of black coal.

"I do not know the man you ask for," he said in stilted English. He turned and hobbled away, using the stick as a cane. He entered the dark adobe hut and pulled a buffalo hide across the adobe entrance.

"What was that all about?" Ned asked.

Tom Beck shrugged his shoulders. "I guess he doesn't know Charlie Killbuck."

"Or he won't tell us if he does," Ned said. "I thought you said the Cherokees were friendly."

"They are. We'll try someone else."

"Are you sure Lina Miller said she was coming to Tishomingo?"

"Yeah, maybe you misunderstood her, Tom," Frank Shaw offered. "Maybe Charlie Killbuck doesn't live here."

"No, dammit," Beck said. "Lina said Tishomingo and when I told her I'd been here before, she described the valley to me. This is the place. I think that old man's spent too many days in the sun. I think his brains have shriveled up with age." He reined his horse to the left. "Come on, let's find someone else."

Beck led the way this time. He didn't bother to stop and call out to the shepherd boy who was in the midst of a small flock of sheep out in the field, and too far away to hear him. Instead, they rode some distance to the next adobe where two Cherokee women were busy at the outdoor fire ring near their hut.

Both women wore buckskin dresses that were decorated with colorful beadwork. The one who stirred the contents of the big black kettle was older and heavier then the pretty, young girl who knelt by a flat rock and kneaded a lump of thick dough. The two women had long black hair. The older woman's hair hung loose about her flat, puffy face. The girl wore her hair in a long braid that fell to the middle of her back. She also wore a bright red ribbon at the top of her braid, as if to hold it in place.

Remington figured them to be mother and daughter. He knew both women had been watching them.

When the lawmen stopped nearby, the women turned away and went back to their chores.

Tom Beck called out a greeting in Cherokee.

The older woman stopped stirring and looked up at Beck, the ladle poised in her hand. The younger girl rested her sticky hands on the dough and turned her head toward them.

"No English," the older woman replied, even though Beck had spoken to them in their native tongue.

Beck continued to speak in the gutteral Cherokee language, explaining that they were looking for a man called Charlie Killbuck and that they had come to help the girl who was with him, Lina Miller.

"No," the older woman said curtly. She turned away and began to stir the pot again. The younger girl hesitated only a minute before she, too, turned her head and went back to her kneading.

"We aren't going to get anywhere with them," Beck said. "Let's go."

"Something funny's going on here," Remington said.

"What do you mean?" Beck snapped. "Just because the old man's too old to think straight, and the two women don't want to talk to strangers? I don't see anything funny about that."

Remington, sensing Tom's frustration, let it go. Tom got moody sometimes and Ned didn't want to deal with that right now.

They stopped at the next adobe, but they couldn't find anyone there. When they left there, Ned spotted an Indian on horseback on the road ahead of them. "Let's catch up to that fellow," he said. "Maybe he'll be kind enough to take us to Killbuck's place."

The deputies urged their horses to a faster pace. When they were closer to the lone, bronze-skinned rider, Tom Beck called out to him, both in English and Cherokee. The Indian, who rode bareback on the pony, looked back over his shoulder, then stopped his animal and waited until the marshals caught up with him.

Remington and Frank Shaw held back a few feet and let Beck do the talking. Remington saw that the Cherokee boy was young, maybe twenty, maybe only eighteen. He wore moccasins and a breechclout, and tucked into his breechclout was a scabbard which held a knife. He had no other weapons.

Beck spoke to the lad in Cherokee and the only words Remington understood were "Charlie Killbuck." The boy shook his head and replied in his native tongue. Beck questioned him further, mentioning the name Lina. Again the boy shook his head and replied in Cherokee. Beck wouldn't let up and within minutes, the two were involved in a heated argument.

Not understanding a word of it, Remington looked over at Frank Shaw and shrugged his shoulders. Shaw smiled and shook his head.

Beck pointed to his own deputy's badge as he spoke, then made a wide sweeping gesture with his arm, indicating the entire valley of Tishomingo.

"Killbuck, yes," the Indian lad said with a nod, and then he shook his head vigorously and rattled off more gutteral words. He tapped the handle of his sheathed knife with two fingers, then doubled up his fist and pounded on his bare chest as if he were plunging a knife into his heart.

A few more heated words were exchanged in Cherokee and then Beck said, "Go on. Go on," and waved the boy on.

"What's the problem?" Remington asked. "Is Killbuck here?"

Beck sighed deeply and watched the boy ride away. "Killbuck lives here in the valley, but that's all I could get out of the boy. I don't know if Killbuck and the girl are here now or not."

"Well, we'll just keep looking until we find them," Remington said.

"It's not going to be that simple," Beck said with a scowl. "It seems like Paco Gaton and his friend Haskins rode through here four or five days ago looking for Killbuck and Lina Miller."

"That's not good," Remington said.

"Fortunately, Charlie Killbuck and the girl weren't here at the time. And when Killbuck got here and found out about the Mexican and the mean-looking white man who were looking for him, he told his people not to give out any information about him or the girl to any strangers who passed through. That's why we've gotten the cold shoulder from these people."

"I can understand that," Remington said, "but didn't you tell him we were lawmen and we wanted to help Lina?"

"Yes, I did, but it didn't do any good. That's what we were arguing about. Killbuck told them not to say anything about him to strangers and to these people, we're strangers, badge or no badge."

"Why was that boy pointing to his knife and pounding on his chest?" Frank Shaw asked. "For a minute I thought he was going to kill you."

Beck smiled. "He said that his people would rather die by their own hands than betray a brother. The Cherokees are fiercely loyal people and we aren't going to learn a damned thing from them."

Chapter Four

Remington was disappointed that they were so close to finding Lina Miller, and yet, so far away. And now that he knew that the men who had murdered her father had tracked the girl to this valley, he was more concerned for her safety than he was in finding her for the purpose of taking her back to Galena. Paco Gaton and Norville Haskins would kill her if they found her first. He had no doubts about that.

He looked out across the land and focused on the obscure buildings near the river front as he considered all the aspects of their situation.

"If the Cherokees won't tell us where Charlie Killbuck lives," he said, "maybe the white men who live near the river can help us."

"They might," Tom Beck said as he looked toward the river.

"If not, I think we'd better push on and start tracking Gaton and Haskins," Ned said.

"Maybe we'll get lucky," Frank Shaw said as he scratched his itching chin through the wiry hairs of his thick, gray beard. "Maybe those river rats can give us a lead on Gaton and Haskins."

"Oh, sure, Frank," Remington said. "And maybe

while they're at it, they'll tell us exactly where Peter Van Hook's ranch is. And maybe it'll snow in hell."

The three men laughed and the tension seemed to drain away from them.

"If nothing else," Beck said, "I know of a little place down on the river front where we can get some good smoked fish. I ate there when I came through here before."

"What are we waiting for, then?" Shaw said. "I'm starved."

"Maybe food will improve our moods," Ned said. He touched his bootheel to his horse's side and snapped the reins. As the three deputies rode through the quiet pasture land, Ned knew that they were being observed by the Cherokees. He saw the Indians in the fields stop their work and watch them pass by. The people near the adobe huts paused from their chores long enough to openly stare at the riders. And the shepherds among the flocks of white sheep looked their way.

"Tom, I thought this was the Chickasaw Nations," he said.

"It is, just north of here," Beck said. "Some of the Cherokees from Tahlequah immigrated down here to raise their sheep so they'd be closer to the shipping waters of the Red. I hear that some of them have drifted as far south as the Brazos."

"Look at that odd rock formation," Ned said, interrupting Beck. He gestured off to his right. "It looks like a big devil's den, if you look at it just right."

"It'd make a good hiding place," Frank Shaw said. "You want to check it out?"

"No, it's too far away," Remington said. "If Lina and her uncle were hiding there, they'd be gone before we could ride over there. Let's just keep going."

The dusty road, rutted with the tracks of wagon wheels, led straight to the small river front town. When they got there, Remington realized that there were more buildings nestled among the cottonwoods than he'd first thought. The small homes he saw were scattered out and well away from the main part of the town. Some were made from adobe, but most of them were crude shacks put together with rough, uneven slabs of wood.

As they turned onto the busy, dirt road of the small town, Ned reined his horse up in the shade of a clump of trees and looked down at the wide river.

"This place is bigger than I thought," he said as the other two men stopped beside him.

"It's a busy port," Beck said.

There were three boats docked in the small harbor. One of them was nothing more than an empty hulk of a raft with wooden plank sides. Another looked like a fishing boat. The third boat was the one with all the action around it. Bare-chested dock workers, wearing bands around their heads to keep the sweat from running down into their eyes, loaded heavy bundles of the white shearings from the sheep into the boat. Loose balls of the white fleece littered the dock and the area around it where some men sat on kegs in the shade and watched the proceedings.

"That's the ferry we'll take to cross the river," Beck said, indicating the empty hulk of the wooden raft. "Then we'll have a lot of land to cover before we reach the other part of the river where another ferry will take us across to the Red River Station."

"And hopefully, Van Hook's ranch," Ned sighed. "This smells like a river town, doesn't it?" He could smell the aroma of cooking fish, but he also smelled the dankness of the town, the stench of rotting waste and animal droppings.

"I've smelled worse," Frank Shaw said.

"Where's this smoked fish place, Tom?" Ned asked as he looked down the busy dirt road that was about a block long and lined with the weather-beaten buildings of the town.

"At the other end of the street," Beck said.

As the trio rode along the crowded street, Remington made a mental note of everything he saw. The mercantile store, a meat market, a blacksmith's stall, a dilapidated building called Traders Center, several nondescript wooden structures that butted up to each other. There was even a small hotel with a wooden sign above the door that bore the name: River Front Hotel. A smaller sign to the left of the door read: Baths, 25 cents. Clean towel, 5 cents. Small clusters of the white sheep's fleece, apparently blown up from the dock, stuck to everything.

Some of the townspeople ignored them completely. Others looked up as they rode past, and those who noticed their shiny badges, watched them with idle curiosity.

Remington took note of every face he saw, hoping for a glimpse of Paco Gaton and Norville Haskins. Tom Beck had furnished him with the description of the two men as he had gotten it from Lina Miller. Gaton was a short Mexican who carried a knife and a Colt .45. He had a moustache and an ugly scar across one cheek that Lina figured had been caused by a knife wound. Haskins was a tall man, muscular, with dark, beady eyes, an ugly pinched face, clean shaven, and long dark hair, dirty hair, Lina had said, that stuck out from his hat. Haskins was lean and had rounded shoulders, according to Lina.

"This is it," Beck said as he pulled back on his reins and dismounted.

Ned glanced at the cafe and smelled the aroma that escaped from the black kettle that had been made into a crude fish smoker. The smoker sat in front of the cafe, off to the side.

The cafe was small and Remington could tell by looking through the windows that it was crowded. There were three tables and benches outside, in front of the cafe, and two of them were occupied. The pretty woman and two gentlemen who sat at one table had not yet been served. At the other table, a big lumbering hulk of a man sat alone and ate the fish and chunks of fried potatoes with his hands. He looked like a dock worker and wore an unbuttoned shirt that showed part of his large, well-tanned chest.

As Ned and Frank dismounted, an elderly man wearing a stained apron emerged from the cafe. He carried a platter in one hand and long tongs in the other. He smiled when he saw them.

"Come in, come in," said the jolly cook as he walked toward the smoker. "I've got fresh fish just for you." He set the platter down on a sidebar. When he opened the smoker, a cloud of smoke and steam billowed up.

"Smells good," Ned said. He felt suddenly weak with hunger.

The cook used the tongs to pluck some fish from the smoker and stack it on the platter, then quickly replaced the lid. He carried the platter to the lady and two gentlemen who were waiting for it, then turned and motioned for Ned and his group to come and eat.

"You can sit right here," said the cook, motioning to the empty table, "or you can go on inside the cafe where it's a mite cooler."

"Is there anywhere we can water our horses first?" Remington asked.

"There shore is," said the cook. "You just take 'em out back and hitch 'em up in the shade of the trees. I keep a watering trough out there for my customers' horses. There's a barrel of grain there, too, if you need it."

"Thanks," Remington said. "We'll be right back."

"Only a dollar a piece for all you can eat," the cook beamed.

The three deputies led their horses around behind the cafe and tethered the animals to the long ropes that had been provided. They dumped some grain in three of the empty buckets they found and set them out.

"Do you think our saddlebags will be safe out here?" Remington said.

"We won't be gone long, Ned," Beck said. "Let's leave them here."

"Yeah," said Shaw. "We can eat at the outside table and keep an eye out. If anyone walks toward the back, we'll see them."

"Well, take your rifles with you." Remington dug the three warrants out of his inside coat pocket and stuffed them into his pants pocket.

"What do you need those for?" Shaw asked.

"I'm not going to leave them here. I want them in my possession." Ned looked all around and didn't see anyone. He knew that Shaw was right. Since the cafe was the last building on the street, they would see anyone who started around toward the back.

"You ready to eat?" the cook said with a big grin as they walked back to the front.

"Yes, we'll eat out here in the fresh air," Ned said. He sat down at the empty table where he could watch both the street and the side of the cafe. Tom and Frank sat on the bench across from him. From there they could look through the windows of the cafe and they could also watch the side of the building. They all set their rifles down close by their sides.

"You want fried potatoes with your fish?" the cook asked.

"Of course," Beck said with a smile. "I never tasted potatoes as good as the way you fix them."

"Oh, you've eaten here before?"

"Once. A year ago, but I'm sure you don't remember me."

The cook tilted his head back and looked at Tom Beck for a minute. "Can't say as I do," he said. "You fellows want beer?"

"No. Have you got coffee?" Remington asked.

"Yep. Black and strong," the cook answered.

"Just the way we like it," Remington said.

"I'll be back in a minute," the cook said and then went into the cafe.

Ned studied the faces of four men who emerged from the tavern across the street. They didn't look his way as they headed down the street and none of them fit the description of the men he was searching for. He looked over at the big man at the next table. The fellow glanced briefly at Ned, as if to say he didn't like being stared at, then continued to eat the fish with his dirty hands. He sloshed the food down with a big gulp of beer and paid no attention to the lawmen.

The cook returned to Ned's table carrying a heavy

tray. He set the tray on the table and then placed a clean plate, a linen napkin and silverware in front of each of the men. He handed each of them a steaming cup of coffee, then set a platter heaped with fried potatoes in the middle of the table. He walked over to the smoker and came back with another platter loaded with smoked fish.

"Hope you enjoy your food," he said.

"We will," Beck assured him.

"Are you fellows here in town on official business?" the friendly cook asked.

"Sort of," Remington said. "Do you know any of the Indians who live near here?"

"A few of them," the cook said. "They don't ever eat here, but sometimes they'll come in and buy smoked fish to take home."

"Do you know Charlie Killbuck?" Tom Beck asked. He picked up the platter of fish, scooped a few pieces on his plate and passed it to Shaw, then helped himself to the potatoes.

"Yeah, I know Charlie Killbuck," the cook said with a big grin. And then a worried expression came over his face. "Charlie ain't in trouble, is he?"

"No," said Beck. "We just want to talk to him. You know where he lives?"

"No, I wouldn't know that," the cook said. "The Indians come to the river front to do their business, but we don't ever ride out to their village. It's sort of an unwritten law around here."

"Do you know a fellow by the name of Norville Haskins?" Remington asked as he took the platter from Shaw and slid some fish onto his plate. "He rides with a Mexican, Paco Gaton." He glanced again at the big man at the next table. The dock worker was pouring another glass of foamy beer from a pitcher and didn't see Ned looking his way.

The cook thought a minute. "Can't say as I do."

"How about a man named Peter Van Hook?" Remington said with a mouthful of fish. "This is good."

"Thanks." The cook scratched his chin, wrinkled his brow. "Van Hook, Van Hook. He's a rancher, ain't he?"

"Yes," said Ned.

"He's got a big spread south of the border, don't he?"

"Yes, that's the one," Ned said. He continued to watch the side of the building as he ate and listened to the elderly cook.

"Yeah, he's been in here a time or two," the cook said with a scowl. "But, I gotta tell you, I don't much like him."

"Why's that?" Beck asked. He forked a couple of chunks of fried potatoes and put them in his mouth.

"He comes in here wearin' his fancy duds and starts demanding things I don't have."

"Like what?" Frank Shaw asked.

"Like beefsteak and beans and corn muffins to go with his fish. Hell, this is a smoked fish place, not a fancy restaurant. He wants beefsteak, he can go on up the street to the restaurant next to the hotel. I told him that, but he insists I trot up there and get it for him. I don't, though, you can bet on that."

"What does he look like?" Remington asked, still chewing.

"Like I say, he wears fancy clothes. A suit and tie, a white hat. Spit an' polished boots. He's got long blond hair, slicked back, parted in the middle. He's nice looking, I reckon, but I don't trust a man with eyes like that."

"What's wrong with his eyes?" Beck asked.

"Nothin'. They're just blue and cold and empty, and they give me the creepy crawlies whenever he looks at me. It's like I never know what he's a-thinkin.' I knowed a killer with eyes like that one time and it was like nobody was home back there."

"Has he been here recently?" Ned asked.

"Naw, I ain't seen him in a coupla weeks."

"What's your name?" Remington asked the cook.

"Mike. Mike Madonna," the cook said proudly.

"Well, thanks, Mike. You've been a big help, and your fish is delicious."

"Well, thank you, sir," Madonna nodded. "If you need more fish or potatoes, let me know."

"We've still got plenty left. Thanks."

"If you're gonna stick around town, I'd suggest you stay at the hotel," Mike said. "A dollar a night and you get clean sheets."

"Thanks," Remington said. "After sleeping on the hard ground for a week, my weary bones could use a comfortable bed."

"My brother owns the hotel. Tell him I sent you."

"We'll do that, Mike."

The cook walked to the nearby table and collected the money from the big man who had just pushed his plate away and taken a last swill of beer. After the fellow left, Mike started to clear the table.

Remington watched the big man stroll across the street and enter the tavern. He stopped Madonna as the cook walked by with a load of dirty dishes.

"Do you know that fellow who was sitting there?" Ned nodded toward the cleared table.

Madonna glanced back at the table. "Harvey? Yeah, I know him. He eats here a coupla times a week."

"Is he a dock worker?"

"Sometimes. When the fish aren't biting."

"Oh, he's a fisherman?"

"Most of the time. If the weather's bad, he does odd jobs around town."

"Do you buy your fish from him?" Tom Beck said.

"Oh, no. My two sons catch all the fish I use," Mike answered proudly. "Harvey sells his fish to the folks downstream from here."

"Just curious," Remington said.

"I suppose it's the nature of your job," Mike said as he nodded and walked away with the dirty dishes.

Remington finished eating what was on his plate and when Frank Shaw passed him the platter of fish, he waved it away.

"No, thanks. I'm full," he said. He took a final drink of coffee, stood up and fished a five-dollar bill out of his pocket and slid it across the table to Tom Beck. "Pay Mike when you're through eating." He picked up his rifle.

"Where are you going?" Beck asked.

"I'm going to check on the horses. You two take your time."

"You aren't getting fidgety, are you, Ned?" Shaw asked.

Remington smiled. "No. We've been in the saddle so long, I just need to stretch my legs for a while. Go ahead and finish your meal."

He walked around the side of the cafe. Yes, he was getting fidgety. He knew it and so did his men. He didn't like leaving the horses and their gear unattended. Besides the extra ammunition, they didn't carry anything of much value in their saddlebags. Food, cooking utensils, extra food, field glasses, knives, things like that. But he didn't like the thought of anyone going through their things.

He felt relieved when he walked around back and saw all three horses back in the shade of the trees. He checked the buckets and saw that the animals had eaten their fill.

"Hello, boy," he said as he walked up to his Missouri trotter. "Did you get enough to eat?" He patted the horse on the neck.

He saw the movement out of the corner of his eyes. Just above the saddle. He whirled his head around and saw the pistol come up over the saddle. At the same instant, the man holding the pistol popped up from behind Ned's horse.

Remington's heart skipped a beat. His muscles tautened.

"Are you the one who's looking for Charlie Killbuck?" the stranger asked as he aimed the pistol at Remington's head.

Chapter Five

Startled by the ambusher, Ned Remington froze in place. He caught his breath and felt his knees go weak. His heart pounded wildly in his chest, but on the outside, he appeared calm. There was no look of surprise on his face as he faced his attacker. There was no trembling in his hand when he removed it from his horse's neck and held it shoulder high, fingers loosely spread. His rifle, still clutched in his left hand, was pointed toward the ground and he knew it would be awkward to swing it up and aim it at the man who had been hiding behind his horse.

The chief deputy marshal had half-way expected to find Paco Gaton or Haskins, or one of their henchmen, messing with the horses. But this stranger was an Indian, and that surprised Ned almost as much as the fact that he was there in the first place. He could only see the ambusher from the shoulders up, but it was enough for Ned to know that he was Indian, even though he was not bare-chested as the others had been. This man wore a tan shirt, open at the collar, and a wide-brimmed hat, pulled low, so that Ned could just barely see his dark eyes, the high cheekbones, the bronze color of his face and neck, the dark skin of the hand that held the pistol.

Remington considered his chances of going for his own pistol, but he had no idea how good this Indian was with a gun.

"What do you want?" the lawman asked, his voice calm, even. He let his arm drop slowly, then eased his hand down toward his holstered pistol.

"Do not try it, marshal," the Indian warned.

Remington's hand hovered above the butt of his pistol, but he didn't move it any closer. He stood perfectly still and looked at the ambusher.

"Are you looking for Killbuck?" the Indian asked, his voice low and demanding.

"Yes, but we mean him no harm," Remington said. He squinted his eyes against the blinding spot of sunlight that glinted and danced off the barrel of the man's pistol, and found himself staring down the dark, ominous hole that was aimed between his eyes. He didn't move a muscle.

"I know," the Indian said.

Ned was confused. Why was this man here if he knew that Remington meant no harm to any of his people?

"We want to help the girl who is with Killbuck," he said, not taking his eyes off the pistol that rested on top of his saddle, not more than four feet away.

"I am Charlie Killbuck," the Indian said in a hushed voice. He slowly withdrew the pistol and slid it down, out of sight.

"You're Killbuck?" Ned said.

"Yes. My people tell me you are looking for me."

"We came to help Lina Miller." The pounding in

Remington's chest slowed and he felt his breathing return to almost normal. Still, he did not move.

"I know," said Killbuck. He looked around nervously, his head twisting back and forth, his dark brown eyes shifting in their sockets.

Charlie Killbuck eased around the back end of Remington's horse and Ned saw that the Cherokee wore dark trousers and boots that were common to the white man. He finally let his arm drop to his side and began to relax as the Indian came around and stood a few feet away, facing him.

"That is why I came to find you before you went away," Killbuck said in a whispered voice. "I have much to tell you about Van Hook and the murdering thieves who work for him."

"What about Lina?" Ned asked. "Is she all right?"

Killbuck glanced in both directions. "We cannot talk here," he whispered. "I will ride back to my village now. You and your men come."

"With you?" Remington asked.

"No. You wait. Someone might see us if we ride together. You come after I am there."

"Where will we find you?" Ned asked.

Killbuck stepped closer. "I will be at my adobe. It is near the road. I will see you when you come."

"Is Lina there?"

"I must go now. You come." Killbuck turned and quickly went around behind Ned's horse. He darted in among the trees and soon disappeared through the thick foliage.

Ned stood there for a minute and took a deep breath. He thought he heard the pounding of hoofbeats as they faded away, but he couldn't quite distinguish the sound from the other noises of the busy river front town. He thought about going around front to tell his partners of the news, but he decided against it. Frank and Tom would be there soon enough and if they were being watched, the less activity, the better.

He slipped his rifle back in the sheath that hung from his saddlehorn, then checked all three horses, tightened the cinches of the saddles where they needed it. He made sure that all of the saddlebags were still secure. He untied his horse from the long tether and was sitting atop his saddle when the other two deputies came around back.

"You ready to go?" Shaw asked.

"Whenever you are," Remington said.

"Are we going to do some more checking here in town?" Tom Beck asked.

"Not now."

"Are we going to head across the river?" Shaw asked.

"Not now," Ned said again.

The two deputies looked at each other and shrugged their shoulders. They sheathed their rifles, checked their horses, untied the animals from the tethers, then climbed up in their saddles.

"You lead the way, Ned," Shaw said as he took the reins in his hand.

Remington glanced over at the tavern as he and his men rode around to the front of the cafe. He wished the curtains at the tavern windows were open so he could look inside as they rode by. It looked like a place where he could get some information if the barkeep was willing to talk. He'd save it for later. Right now, he had more important things to do.

As they rode back through the small river front town, he once again studied the faces of the people he saw. And again, he got the impression that nobody was particularly impressed or bothered by the fact that three lawmen were in their town.

After they passed the last building on the short street, Ned tugged the reins to the right and turned on to the road that would take them back to the Indian village.

"Where are we going?" Beck asked.

Remington glanced back at Tom. "I'll tell you later."

The big man sat at a table at the front of the tavern, next to one of the windows. He peered out through the flimsy material of the curtains and saw the three lawmen ride around to the street from the back of the cafe. He'd been sipping at a beer and watching out the window ever since he'd come in here, right after he'd finished eating his fish and potatoes.

He saw the tallest of the deputies glance over at the tavern, but he knew the lawman couldn't see through the curtains. Not even enough to see his big shadow sitting there by the window. It was bright outside that afternoon and, with the curtains closed, the tavern was dark and gloomy.

After the lawmen rode on down the street, the big man got up from the table and walked out the batwing doors. He paused for a minute, and let his eyes adjust to the bright sunlight, then strolled out far enough so he could see the backs of the three deputies as they rode away from him.

Those stupid bastards are incompetent, or inexperienced, he thought as he watched them go. They didn't even stop anywhere else in town to ask questions, and they sure as hell hadn't learned anything new from Mike Madonna. Mike didn't know anything. Hell, if he were in their shoes, the first place he'd stop and ask questions in any town would be the tavern or the saloon. Barkeeps were notorious for knowing a lot of facts about a lot of folks and from his own experience, he knew that most barkeeps would spill their guts for a price.

When the lawmen turned right at the end of the street, he wondered where they were going. Probably back to the Cherokee village to look for the half-breed girl, he figured. Well, they wouldn't find her. They were too dumb.

He'd been watching for two weeks now for some sign of the half-breed girl and Charlie Killbuck, or any lawman who came to town. The two outlaws had told him they'd pay him for such information, and he considered himself lucky that he'd been eating at the fish place when the deputies stopped there. It was a coincidence, he knew, and he took it as a sign that his luck was finally changing for the better. He considered himself even more fortunate that he'd been sitting close enough to listen in on the conversation when the marshals were questioning Mike.

He thought about following the lawmen, but decided against it. He had enough information for now and he was in a hurry. Besides, the deputies would be staying at the River Front Hotel that night. He had heard them tell Madonna as much, and he would pass that information along.

He faced an hour's ride down the river in his fishing boat to the small harbor where the two outlaws were staying, and it was a trip he was looking forward to. When he got there, he would be paid handsomely when he delivered the information he had to Paco Graton and Norville Haskins.

Harvey Cardin just wished that the cook had been able to supply the lawmen with Killbuck's whereabouts. He wanted to know, too. That would have been the capper he needed to prove to Gaton and Haskins that he was not a loser. But the two outlaws would be happy with what he told them and he would do anything he could to help them.

Harvey swelled his chest out. Nobody could call him dumb anymore. He knew where the easy money was, and he intended to get all of it he could.

Chapter Six

Ned Remington almost missed seeing Charlie Killbuck. The Cherokee stood just inside the doorway of his adobe, where it was dark and shadowy. Ned had already explained to his two deputies about his encounter with Killbuck and all three of the lawmen had been studying the huts they passed for some sign of the Indian who had promised to talk to them.

Charlie Killbuck stepped out of the shadows when the lawmen slowed near his adobe. He came out of his hut cautiously and scanned the long, deserted road that stretched back to the river front. The short Cherokee Indian still wore the tan shirt and dark trousers and the wide-brimmed hat he'd worn in town. His pistol was snugged into the holster that rode high on his leg, within easy reach.

"You were not followed here, were you?" he asked nervously.

"No," said Remington. He glanced back at the road and realized that it was later in the day than he'd thought. Long shadows from the few trees along the way now stretched ominously across the road. "Nobody seemed to pay much attention to us in town, and I certainly wouldn't have risked coming here if we were being tailed. I checked our back trail often enough to know that we weren't followed."

"Good. I knew you would be careful."

"These are my two deputies," Ned said. "Tom Beck and Frank Shaw. Beck is the one who rode to Osage, Arkansas, and talked to Lina after her father and her uncle were murdered."

"Yes, Frank Twokill was my brother." Killbuck looked up at the deputy who was part Cherokee. "I am glad you are here. Lina said you would come and help us find those bastards who killed Frank and Woody, then stole their cattle."

"Where is Lina?" Beck asked as he peered at the doorway of the darkened adobe.

"First, we talk," Killbuck said. "Come. Follow me." He gestured with a wave of his arm. "We put your horses in the shed out back where they cannot be seen. We talk out there."

Charlie Killbuck walked around to the back of his adobe hut. As Ned and his deputies followed on horseback, Ned looked out at the small flock of sheep in the pasture which was some fifty yards beyond the shed and the other outbuildings. A young shepherd boy, dressed in dark trousers and shirt and wearing a hat like Killbuck's, stood in the midst of the white sheep. The boy was dressed like the other shepherds they'd seen and some of the other Cherokees besides Killbuck had been dressed in the white man's clothes, as well. Ned noticed that the shepherd boy was watching them.

"Are those your sheep out there?" Remington asked with a nod of his head.

"Yes," Killbuck said. "I do not have as many sheep as I had before, but I will build my flock back up after Paco Gaton and Haskins are brought to justice."

"Is that your son out there tending the sheep?" Ned asked.

"No." Killbuck shook his head sadly. "I have no son. I have no family of my own. Only Lina and my dead brother's wife and her two small children. My own wife died many moons ago and the great spirit above took our unborn child with her."

"I'm sorry," Ned said.

Killbuck looked up at the cloudless sky and held his open palm out. "If the rain does not come soon, the grasses will die and that will be bad for the sheep," he said, as if to change the subject. "It will be bad for all of the people in Tishomingo." He walked on into the crude stable and motioned for the others to follow.

Remington smelled the heavy stench of horse droppings as he approached the stable. He ducked his head as he rode through the archway of the open door, even though the opening was plenty tall enough to accommodate a man on horseback. The other end of the shed was open, too, and once he was inside, it took no time at all for Remington's eyes to adjust to the dimmer light of the small stable. He noticed the two Indian ponies in separate stalls and hoped one of them belonged to Lina Miller.

Both of the spotted ponies cocked their ears, raised their heads, at the sound of the intruding men. Their rubbery nostrils flared as they caught the scent of the strange horses.

"Tie your horses here," Killbuck said, tapping the short rail in the middle of the stable. "We go outside to talk, where we can watch the trail."

The three lawmen dismounted and tied their horses to the hitchrail, then followed Killbuck outside, where the Indian once again checked the road to town.

"What can you tell us about Paco Gaton and Norville Haskins?" Remington asked.

"They have bad spirits," Killbuck said. He spit on the ground with disgust. "They steal many, many cattle. They kill many ranchers. When I learned of the trouble at Woody Miller's ranch, I ride to Osage. I talk to many people. I tracked the stolen cattle back down to the stockyard at the Red River Station across the border. In Texas. The man who runs the stockyard, Rupert Smith, he tells me the cattle belong to Mr. Peter Van Hook, but I know better."

"Five hundred head are a lot of beeves to take across the Red by ferry," Frank Shaw said.

"No, they do not take by ferry." Killbuck looked over at the gray-haired deputy. "The cattle ford the Arkansas River and the Red at places where the water is not so wide."

"Do you know where Van Hook lives?" Remington asked.

"No, but I think near the Red River Station. Lina wants to go down there and kill all of them. I tell her it is too dangerous, but she does not care. She wants revenge. Eye for an eye."

"Killbuck, I want to send Lina back to Galena," Remington said. "Tom Beck will take her back and see to her safety."

"I want that, too, but Lina will not go." Killbuck shook his head. "She will not leave until her father's murderers are brought to justice."

"But it's too dangerous for her to be here so close to the border," Remington said.

"I know. I tell Lina that, but she does not listen. I told her to stay in Osage and let the law take care of the murderers. But she says that Gaton and Haskins saw her and that it is more dangerous for her to stay in Osage where they can find her."

"But we want to take her to Galena, where she'll be safe," Remington explained.

"You talk to her," Killbuck said. "Maybe she will listen to you."

"Where is she?" Remington asked.

Killbuck nodded toward the pasture. "She is the shepherd tending my flock."

"That's Lina?" Remington said, the surprise showing in his voice.

"Yes. She stays out there all day where she can watch the trail. You men go outside my adobe house. Go in the back door and wait in the parlor. I will bring Lina in."

As Charlie Killbuck headed out to the pasture, the three lawmen entered his small adobe hut. They walked through the kitchen and past two tiny bedrooms before they found the neat, sparsely furnished parlor. When they walked into the room, Ned smelled the delicate aroma of a woman's perfume, the hint of woodsmoke from an old fire in the fireplace. The curtains at the windows were open and the room was bright with the late afternoon sunlight.

A tattered sofa sat in the middle of the room. Facing the sofa were two equally tattered, upholstered chairs, and in between the sofa and the chairs was a low table. Bookcases, fashioned from wooden crates, lined one wall. A straight chair and a dressing table,

also made from crates, sat in one corner of the room.
A brush, comb, hand mirror and several small bottles
and jars were neatly arranged on the dressing table,
and above the table, a framed mirror hung on the
wall. A worn carpet covered most of the dirt floor.
Beyond the parlor was the entry hall where Killbuck
had waited in the shadows of the doorway for their
arrival.

Frank Shaw sat down on the sofa. "Feels good to
be out of the saddle," he said as he removed his hat
and ran his fingers through his gray locks of hair.

"I agree," Tom Beck said. He flexed weary muscles before he plunked down next to Shaw.

Remington strolled around the room and looked at
the Indian artifacts, then paused at the bookshelves.
He pulled out a cloth-bound book on the Cherokee
Nations and thumbed through it. "It looks like Charlie
Killbuck is an educated man," he said.

He was still browsing through the books a few
minutes later when he heard the back door open and
close. He put the book he was holding back on the
bookshelf, then walked to the middle of the room. He
took his hat off just as Killbuck and the girl entered
the room.

"This is my niece, Lina Miller," Killbuck announced.

"Hello, Lina," Tom Beck said as he stood up and
removed his hat. Shaw stood, too.

"Hello, Marshal Beck," Lina said in a soft voice.
"Thank you for coming."

With hat in hand, Ned stepped forward. "I'm Ned
Remington, U.S. Deputy Marshal," he said. "You already know Tom Beck, and the other fellow over
there is Deputy Frank Shaw."

"Hello," Lina said as she nodded to each man. "I saw you ride through the village earlier today."

When the girl looked up at him with her deep blue eyes, Ned saw that she was indeed, as Judge Barnstall had said, very beautiful.

"We're very sorry about your father and your uncle, Lina," he said gently.

"So am I," she said, her lips tight. She reached up and jerked her wide-brimmed hat off, a silent gesture of her anger. Her raven-dark hair tumbled free and fell nearly to her waist.

With her dark skin and deep blue eyes, her high cheekbones, the half-breed girl was a startling beauty and Ned couldn't help but stare at her. The baggy men's clothes she wore concealed her figure, but it couldn't hide her femininity.

"We've come to help you, Lina," he said.

Lina looked directly at Ned, an expression of vindictive challenge in her eyes. "The only way you can help me, Mr. Remington, is to find those awful men who murdered my father and Uncle Frank," she said, a harsh, brittle edge to her voice.

Remington saw the flash of hatred in her bright blue eyes. "We'll find them, miss."

"If you don't, I will," Lina said, a defiant challenge in her voice. "I'll never forget their ugly faces as long as I live. You don't know how much I hate those cold-hearted murderers."

Ned thought of his own daughter, Katy, and what the traumatic experience of seeing her mother killed had done to her. "I do know, Lina," he said.

"No, you don't," Lina said. "Nobody knows how much I hate them." Her voice quavered as she fought back the tears.

Charlie Killbuck put his hand on the girl's shoulder. "Lina, you have to let the law handle this now," he said gently. "Since the murderers saw you and know you can identify them, we all think it's too dangerous for you to be here in Tishomingo, so close to the border. These deputies want to take you to Galena, Missouri, where you'll be safe."

"I won't go, Uncle Charlie," Lina protested. "Not until those evil men are in their graves. With bullet holes in their backs, like Papa and Uncle Frank had." She marched over to the dressing table and slammed her hat down. She sat down on the straight-back chair, scooted it forward, then grabbed the brush and ran it through her long, dark hair.

Remington strolled over to the dressing table and looked down at the girl. "Lina, your uncle's right. It's too dangerous for you here. Tom Beck will escort you to Galena."

"I won't go," she said stubbornly. She glanced up at him with fire in her eyes, then looked in the mirror and brushed her long locks.

As he studied Lina's reflection in the mirror, Ned thought about his own beautiful daughter sitting in her rocking chair, rocking back and forth, mindless because of the tragedy she had witnessed, her eyes vacant of any emotion. He wondered if Katy would have reacted the same way Lina was acting now if Katy hadn't lost her mind because of the shocking horror of the tragic incident.

"Lina, I've got warrants for Paco Gaton and Norville Haskins and we won't give up until we find them," Ned said, shaking the thoughts of Katy from his mind. "When we bring them in, we need you there in Galena to testify in court against these terri-

ble men. That's the only way you can help to make
sure that your father's murderers are brought to justice."

"Brought to justice?" Lina cried out as she looked
up at Ned, the hairbrush poised in her hand like a
dagger.

"Yes, Lina," said Ned calmly. "And with Judge
Samuel P. Barnstall presiding over their trial, you can
be assured that Gaton and Haskins will receive swift
and just punishment."

"Swift and just punishment," Lina snarled, mocking his words. "That's not what I want, Mr. Remington. I want those evil men dead. Right now."

"With your testimony, Gaton and Haskins will
hang," Remington assured her.

"You don't understand anything. None of you do,"
Lina accused. "I want those cruel, heartless men dead
now. They don't deserve a trial."

"Everyone's entitled to a fair trial," Remington
said calmly. "It's the law."

"Well, I don't like your stinkin' laws, marshal," she
snapped. "My father didn't get a fair trial, did he?"

"That's why we're here," Ned said. "That's . . ."

"No. My father didn't get a fair trial," she ranted
on, shaking her brush violently. "Those murdering
thieves killed my father and Uncle Frank in cold
blood and I want those dirty outlaws to suffer the
same kind of cruel treatment."

"The courts will arrange proper punishment for the
criminals," Remington said, knowing full well that
the girl was not listening to him.

"Yes. Punish. Punish," Lina cried, her eyes glazed
over as if she'd been suddenly stricken with madness.
"I want to see the looks on their ugly faces when they

realize they're going to die for their brutal crimes."

"Lina, please listen to me," Remington pleaded in a gentle voice.

He put his hand on her shoulder, but she jerked away and stared up at him as if he were the enemy. She lashed out at him with the hairbrush. Ned grabbed her wrist and warded off the blow.

"I'll kill them myself if I have to," she snarled like a wild animal. "Yes, that's what I'm going to do. Kill. Kill."

Charlie Killbuck and the two deputies stood dumb-founded as they watched the crazed girl.

"Lina, listen to me!" Remington barked harshly. "Stop this nonsense right now." He cuffed her under the chin and roughly tilted her head up so that she was forced to look at him.

Her shoulders slumped and the glazed look faded from her eyes as she snapped out of her hysterical tantrum.

"Lina, please listen to me," Ned said as he re-leased his tight grip on her chin. Still, he kept her head tilted so she had to look at him. "Ted Beck is going to take you to Galena as soon as possible. Do you understand that, Lina?"

"I understand, Mr. Remington. But, I won't go," she said evenly, stubbornly. "I won't go."

Chapter Seven

"I will not go to Galena," Lina said flatly. "I won't go. I understand perfectly well what you're saying, but I won't go."

"You're not listening to me, Lina," the tall chief deputy said. "You must go back to Missouri with Marshal Beck. It's for your own safety."

"It's obvious that you're not listening to me, Mr. Remington," Lina said. "I can't go to Galena right now. I have to stay here and avenge my father's murder. And I plan to do it myself. It's my duty."

Ned Remington knew that even though Lina had calmed down from her hysterical outburst, she still was not thinking clearly. If she'd only use some common sense, she'd know that it would be suicide to go after her father's murderers by herself. But in his line of work, Ned had come to realize that people who had a reason to be emotionally involved in a case didn't always act in a manner that was considered normal.

Lina Miller was reacting to the shock of seeing her father and uncle killed by erupting with a normal outpouring of anger and hatred, coupled with her irrational threats of seeking revenge. Ned wondered if

Lina's impassioned outburst was a healthier means of dealing with grief than the way his own daughter, Katy, had handled it. Not that Katy had chosen her own path, but she had been through a similar tragic situation when she'd witnessed the grim rape and murder of her mother, and then had been brutally raped herself. Katy had buried her grief instead of letting it out. As a result, Katy had become a mind-less zombie, with all of her grief still trapped deep within her.

As he studied the stubborn, defiant, half-breed girl at the dressing table, Remington knew that, in time, Lina Miller would get over her foolish, irrational behavior.

He wasn't so sure about his own Katy. Even though she had been given all the love and tender care that he and the nuns at the convent could possibly give her, Katy would probably spend the rest of her days in that damned rocking chair, staring with vacant eyes at things she was incapable of understanding. With a sinking feeling in the pit of his gut, Ned knew that Katy would never be able to face the horrible truths she'd buried deep inside herself three years ago, the realities of life that waited within her like steel traps that would snap and cut off her life if she allowed herself to think about them. No, Katy would stay in her protective shell where nothing more could hurt her.

At that moment, as he was overwhelmed by his compassion for both of the unfortunate girls, Remington came to realize that his daughter Katy would never be completely well until she could lash out at the world as Lina Miller was doing right now. And with that realization came the first glimmer of hope for Katy that Ned had felt in a long, long time.

A sense of relief flooded through Remington and he felt his taut shoulder muscles begin to relax. He vowed that when he got back to Galena, he would no longer treat his daughter like a delicate china doll. If he could get through to Katy at all, and now he was confident he could, he would do whatever it took to provoke her anger to the point where she would finally have to face the painful horrors that were locked up tight in her heart. It was the only way he knew to bring his darling daughter back into the world of the living.

Ned took a deep breath and let it out slowly as he looked at Lina Miller. The girl's face was flushed beneath her bronzed skin and he realized that he had to be careful what he told her. He had no doubts that, in her present condition, she would not hesitate to ride right into the rustlers' nest with guns blazing. And he knew that if she did, Lina Miller would be killed for her efforts. The poor girl wouldn't stand a chance against such cold-hearted murderers.

Ned shook his head. "Lina, you can't take on Paco Gaton and his friend by yourself."

"I can. And I will." Lina set the brush down, picked up one of the small bottles on the dressing table and dabbed a drop of sweet-smelling perfume behind each ear.

"That would be just plain stupid, Lina. And if your father were alive, he'd be the first one to tell you so. He certainly wouldn't want you risking your life on his account."

"All of your fancy talk isn't going to make me change my mind, Mr. Remington, so save your breath." Lina looked up at Ned. "I'm going after those men and you can't stop me."

"Please don't think that way, Miss Miller," Ned sighed, frustrated by the girl's unreasonable stubbornness. "Can't you understand that we want to help you?"

"I do," Lina said quietly. "But you've got to understand my feelings, too. This is something I have to do."

"We know how you feel, Lina. We really do. It's a very natural thing for you to want to seek revenge."

"It is?"

Lina seemed surprised. Ned saw the intense look in her deep blue eyes and thought he was finally getting through to her.

"Yes, but we won't allow you to risk your life, Lina," he said. "It's our duty as deputy marshals not only to find the men who murdered your father and bring them to justice, but to protect you in the process. Your life is in danger because you witnessed a heinous crime. You must go back to Galena and trust us to take care of the outlaws."

Lina stared down in her lap for a minute, as if she were thinking about what he'd just said. Then she looked up at Remington, more determined than ever.

"I won't go," she said stubbornly. "I'm not afraid of anything."

"Maybe you should be," Ned said sarcastically.

"Why? I can ride and shoot as well as any man alive and if I had been armed that day back in Osage, I would have shot Gaton and Haskins where they stood, instead of running away."

Remington believed her. And he knew he wasn't about to change her mind at the moment. He walked away from the dressing table, hoping the girl would calm down enough to listen to reason. He turned and glanced at Charlie Killbuck.

The Cherokee shrugged his shoulders and shook his head. "Now you learn for yourself how stubborn my niece can be," he said with a sheepish grin. "I have talked to her until my face turns blue."

"And it didn't do you any good, did it, Uncle Charlie?" Lina said with a satisfied smirk.

"No, but I thought you would listen to these lawmen. They know what's best for you."

"I listen only to my heart, as I've been taught," Lina said. "I won't go to Galena until those evil men are in their graves."

"Well, I think we'd better get our tired asses back in the saddle and push on to the Red River Station," Remington said to his men, ignoring the girl. "We sure as hell aren't going to capture those damned bastards standin' here with our thumbs up our butts."

"Why, Mr. Remington! I'm shocked," Lina said.

"At what?"

"Your language. You have a filthy tongue, marshal. That's no way to talk in front of a lady."

"If you consider yourself as tough as a man, then you'd better get used to the language, Miss Miller. It goes with the territory."

Lina didn't reply. She just glared at him for a brief instant, then turned away.

Ned knew what he was doing, but he didn't think it would work with Lina. She was too damned hard-headed for her own good.

"Are you men ready to go?" Remington asked his deputies.

"We're ready," Frank Shaw said with a knowing twinkle in his blue eyes.

"What's the best way to get to the Red River Station?" Ned asked Charlie Killbuck. "Do we take the ferry from the river front?"

"That is a good way to go," said Killbuck, "but I know a better way where no one will see you riding south."

"How's that?" Remington asked.

"I will go with you and show you the way," Killbuck said. "We will go upstream and cross the river where it is not very wide. I will lead you to the Red River Station where you can enquire about Van Hook."

"We'd appreciate that, Killbuck," Ned said as he slid his hat onto his head.

"It would be my honor," Killbuck said with a big grin. "But we must be wary. Paco Graton has friends in the Nations, probably even here in Tishomingo."

"You think so?" Remington asked. He found the news disturbing. He hadn't counted on tangling with Gaton or his men until they were across the border into Texas, and his uneventful trip to the river front town had seemed to confirm those feelings. Now he wondered.

"Yes," Killbuck said. "That is why I was careful when I came looking for you in town. That is why Lina has to dress like a boy. But if we go my way, no one will see us."

Lina reached for her hat and stood up. "I'm going with you," she announced.

"No, you're not, young lady," Remington said in a firm voice. "If you want to stay here, that's your own damned business, but you're not going across the border with us. It'll be too dangerous down there."

Killbuck walked over to the window and looked out. "It is too late in the day to start out anyway," he said. "It would be bad to ride so far at night. Too dangerous. It will be better to go in the morning when you men and your horses are rested."

Remington strolled to the window and looked out at the western sky where the sun seemed to rest briefly on the distant hills.

"I think you're right, Charlie," he said. "We'll wait till morning."

As Ned walked back toward the center of the room, he glanced over at Lina. She glared at him and then pouted as she sat back down and picked up her brush. Even so, he knew she wasn't going to give up without a fight.

"You can stay at the River Front Hotel tonight," Killbuck said. "They have clean rooms and soft beds. We will leave early in the morning."

"That sounds good to me," Frank Shaw said with a deep sigh. "My weary old bones aren't as young as they used to be." He rubbed the small of his back.

"I know what you mean," Killbuck said. "I have done a lot of riding myself lately."

"Don't let him kid you, Killbuck," Tom Beck said. "Shaw may be a crusty old duffer, but he can outride Ned and I put together."

"So could I," Lina said sarcastically, a smug look on her face.

"You come back here at dawn," Killbuck told the deputies. "I will be ready."

"We'll be here. Goodbye, Miss Miller," Ned said as he tipped his hat. "If you change your mind about going to Galena, Marshal Beck will be happy to take you in the morning."

Lina gave Remington a dirty look, but didn't answer.

The sun had already disappeared from the horizon by the time Remington and his men walked out to the shed to get their horses. Killbuck went to the stable with them and again warned the three lawmen that Paco Gaton had friends who could show up anywhere.

The western sky flared with the delicate pink of fresh salmon, then gradually faded to a dull, darkening gray as the three deputies rode back toward the river front town. A few minutes later, as darkness closed in around them, Remington turned his horse off the road without warning and headed for a distant clump of trees he'd been watching.

"Where in the hell are you going, Ned?" Tom Beck called as he reined his horse to the right and followed Remington across the open land.

"I thought we were going to the hotel," Shaw said as he brought his horse in line with the other two.

"No, we're not going anywhere near that town," Ned said. He rode on to the trees and dismounted. "We're going to camp right here tonight."

"Damn, I was looking forward to a nice soft bed," Shaw grumbled.

"Why are we staying here?" Beck asked.

"Two reasons," Ned said. "If Gaton's got friends roaming around this part of the country, then we don't want to show up at the only hotel in town. Especially if news has spread that we're here."

"Makes sense to me," Beck said as he climbed down from his mount.

"Besides, that cook at the fish house suggested that we stay at the River Front Hotel tonight and as far as he knows, that's where we're staying." Ned tethered his horse to one of the trees, using a long hemp rope from his saddlebags so Neal would have room to roam and graze on the summer grasses.

"Madonna?" Beck said. "He doesn't seem like the sort who would be friends with Gaton."

"He said he didn't know Paco Gaton or Haskins," Shaw added. "And it was obvious he didn't like what little he'd seen of Van Hook."

"I know. I liked good ol' Mike," Remington said as the three deputies took care of their horses and unfastened their saddles in the light of the bright stars. The moon, more than half full, was just beginning to rise. "But Madonna's the friendly sort and he could have mentioned our conversation to someone in passing. And there were other folks within earshot when we were talking to Mike."

"Yeah," Shaw laughed. "That beautiful gal who was charming the pants off those two dandies she was with. Damn, she was purty."

"Frank, you've been on the trail too long," Ned said in a teasing voice. "You're not supposed to be gawkin' at the pretty ladies. You're supposed to be payin' attention to business."

"Hell, I'd rather look at a pretty girl than that big ugly brute who was sitting at the next table," Shaw said.

"And that baboon-faced lummox was too busy feeding his face to notice the likes of us," Tom Beck laughed.

"You never know," Ned said after a brief pause,

"but I think we'll all sleep better out here in the open."

"Yeah, if we can sleep with all that racket," Shaw said.

Ned stopped to listen. The sheep in the Indian village had long since bedded down for the night. Dim lights from the adobe huts dotted the land and all was quiet on that front. The faint cacophony of noises came from the opposite direction. It came from the streets of the bustling river front town that glowed with lamplight in the distance. If he listened real hard, he could sort out the musical sounds from a strumming guitar and those from a clinking piano, but the tunes themselves were lost in the distant din of merriment that floated out across the land from the river front saloons.

"A little soft music to put you to sleep, Frank," he said. "The reason I picked this particular spot is because we can see the road from here. If Gaton or his friends decide to go looking for Lina again tonight, we can see them riding by."

"That Lina is a spunky gal, isn't she?" Shaw said as he spread his bedroll out on the ground.

"And stubborn as a mule," Tom Beck said.

"Well, she's gonna find out who's running this show in the morning," Ned said. "There's no way I'm going to take her south to Texas with us."

"I'll bet you end up eating those words," Beck said.

"Not a chance," Ned said.

"I'd be willing to put a little money on it," Beck said with a grin. "That gal's made up her mind she's going with us and I don't think we can stop her."

"Not even your filthy tongue will stop her," Shaw said, mocking the half-breed girl.

The deputies were in a jovial mood. They'd been on the hot dusty trail for a week and they finally felt like they were making progress by finding Lina and Charlie Killbuck.

"Well, she ain't goin' with me," Remington said, dismissing the subject. "We won't build a fire tonight. We'll just eat jerky and hardtack."

"And to think we could be sitting down to a meal of steak and potatoes at this very minute," Shaw said as he glanced toward the glow from the river front. "We're so close to town."

"When you crawl into your bedrolls tonight, keep your weapons handy," Ned said as he spread his own blankets out on the hard ground.

"Are you expecting trouble tonight?" Beck asked in a more serious tone.

"I'm not expecting it," Ned said, "but I didn't like what Killbuck said about Gaton having friends around here. I plan to sleep with one eye open and I think you two should do the same."

Chapter Eight

Ned Remington awoke with a start. He didn't know how long he'd been asleep, but he knew something had awakened him. Something wasn't right.

His eyes shot open and he found himself staring up at the half moon that was already on its downward path toward the western horizon. It had to be way past midnight, probably about two or three in the morning, he figured.

He listened hard and heard only the low, rhythmic snoring of Frank Shaw. During the past week of sleeping out under the stars with his deputies, he'd learned that Tom Beck seldom snored. And during his long years as a marshal when he'd spent many nights sleeping outside, he'd learned to distinguish the ordinary night sounds from those that were out of kilter. Like now.

Other than Frank's snoring, there was only the silence. An ominous silence. No coyotes yapping in the distance, no night birds hooting their calls, no tree leaves flapping in the breeze, no frogs or crickets humming, no music coming from the river front town. There were no sounds of gaiety or drunken voices from the distant saloons.

But something had awakened him. Maybe it was the silence itself that had aroused him from a light sleep. Maybe the saloons had finally closed their doors and the boisterous men at the river front had gone home and gone to bed.

Or maybe it was the bright moonlight suddenly striking his closed eyes that had caused him to come out of a restless sleep. Perhaps the moon had just now reached the point in its travel across the skies where its light shone directly down on his face as he slept on his back, his head turned slightly to the side as it rested on his rolled-up coat.

Remington felt a sudden chill and knew that it wasn't the night air that caused it. The night had been too warm for him to sleep under a blanket and he had stretched out on top of his bedroll, his Henry .44 pistol tucked under his coat pillow, the other pistol nestled between the two blankets under him, near his shoulder. His rifle rested beside him, on top of the blankets. All of the weapons were loaded. Ned had removed his boots, his wide-brimmed hat, and his gunbelt just before he'd stretched out. He had placed the boots and gunbelt just above his head, next to his saddle and saddlebags. He had put his hat on top of the saddle so it wouldn't get any dustier than it already was.

It had taken Ned a long time to fall asleep the night before. Not because the heat of the day had lingered into the late night hours, and not because the noisy din from the saloons had grown louder with the passing hours. It was the result of having a lot on his mind. After he and his men had eaten the jerky and hardtack, and shared a can of cold beans, they had talked for more than an hour before they decided to get some sleep. Ned had used that time to familiarize himself with the darkened landscape, something he always did when he slept on unfamiliar ground.

He knew from their conversation that they were all apprehensive about what they'd be facing the following day, and now that they were getting closer to finding Gaton, Haskins and Peter Van Hook, they were anxious to get moving so they could arrest the two outlaws and the rancher who bought stolen cattle. If Ned's hunches were right, Van Hook was the boss, the top man in the cattle rustling business, and Gaton and Haskins were merely his hired hands, the ones who did Van Hook's dirty work while the rancher raked in the profits.

Remington's main concern, however, had been about Lina Miller. And he thought about her now, as he had done for a long time before he finally fell asleep. He just didn't know what to do with the girl. He still had hopes that she would allow Tom Beck to escort her back to Galena in the morning, but if she refused to go, then he was afraid he'd be forced to take her along with them.

Ned didn't mind giving in to Lina's wishes, but it was just too damned dangerous for her to cross over the border into Texas where she might be spotted by Gaton and his friend. Maybe, if she continued to dress like a boy, she could get away with riding with them without being detected. He felt responsible for the girl's safety, but it was something he'd have to face when they returned to Killbuck's adobe at dawn.

Ned turned his head and glanced over at the other two deputies who were sleeping on top of their own bedrolls, a few feet away. They were also fully dressed except for their boots and they had their weapons within easy reach.

The deputies' horses were tied to the trees, some thirty feet behind them. They made no sound.

Ned didn't want to make any sudden movements in case someone was watching their camp. Better to play possum. He raised his head only slightly and listened again.

Frank Shaw shifted positions in his sleep and the snoring stopped.

Ned held his breath.

The silence that swelled up around him was almost deafening and he could hear his own pulse throbbing in his ears. His pulse had quickened and he could actually feel his heart thumping in his chest. A leg muscle cramped because of Ned's rigid position. He resisted the urge to reach down and rub the pain away. He relaxed the leg as much as he could and waited until the cramp subsided.

Without moving the rest of his body, Ned slowly propped himself up on one elbow and scanned the lonely, moonlit landscape that stretched out in front of him. He saw nothing unusual out there. No movement. No vague silhouettes where they weren't supposed to be. The shadowy outlines of the few dark trees were right where he remembered them to be. The distant contour of the unusual rock formation was just as he had memorized it.

And yet, he sensed something different in the night air. It was almost as if a cloud of doom now hung over them. It was as if the night air had suddenly been charged with tension.

He still had the feeling that something had roused him out of his light sleep. A sound. A smell. A feeling. Otherwise, why had he awakened with such a start? A bad dream, maybe? But he couldn't remember dreaming. Had it been a smell that wasn't familiar to him? He didn't know.

Ned sniffed the night air and drank in the aroma of the dank grasses, the treebark. Even if he couldn't smell the stench from the river front, he could imagine it. The other scents he sniffed out were more familiar to him: the mustiness of the sweaty bedrolls, the leather of the saddles and saddlebags, the bear grease that they used to clean their guns, a hint of gunpowder, the strong aroma of horseflesh. Even the heavy stench of the droppings of the tethered horses was familiar to him, and not unpleasant.

There was a trace of some mustiness in the night air that seemed unfamiliar to him, but he couldn't separate it from the other smells. It smelled almost like human sweat, rank human sweat, he thought. It could be the night-damp fleece of the sheep that he smelled, an odor that he hadn't experienced during the earlier hours of evening. Or it could be the rotting stench of the river town garbage drifting his way. With no breeze, such scents would tend to hover close to the ground.

Dammit, he knew something was out there. He sensed it. And whatever it was had awakened him. Was he the only one who sensed it? Frank Shaw and Ted Beck usually slept as lightly as he did on such outings, and although Shaw had changed positions and stopped snoring, neither man had awakened.

At that moment, Ned Remington felt all alone, apprehensive. It wasn't fear he was experiencing. Ned was never afraid to face danger. Some accused him of having nerves of steel, but he knew better. He had just learned to stay calm and think clearly in tense situations. And that little bit of knowledge and self discipline had saved his ass more than once during his many years as a deputy marshal. The apprehension he was experiencing right now was just an uneasiness over the unknown.

He closed his eyes and strained his ears, listening for any sound at all. All he could hear was his loud heartbeat pounding against his eardrums. His muscles tautened and his leg muscle threatened to cramp up on him again. He forced himself to relax and then eased his leg a few inches to the side so his position wouldn't be so awkward.

Remington was just about to get up and look around when one of the horses behind him suddenly neighed. Ned nearly jumped out of his skin.

He whirled his head around, strained his neck, and looked back at the horses that were tied to the trees. Another of the three horses that belonged to the lawmen whinnied and all three animals cocked their ears toward the wagon-rutted road that stretched between the river front and the Indian village. Their rubbery nostrils flared as they sniffed the night air.

So I wasn't imagining things, Ned thought as he snapped his head back around and peered in the direction of the road.

And then he saw them. Not more than fifty yards away. Five horsemen looming out of the shadows of darkness, riding toward the Indian village. Ned spotted the riders just in time to see them rein up hard at the sound of the whinnying horses. The riders' horses rared back, their front hooves pawing the air until the horses dropped their legs and skidded to a halt. Even though it was fairly dark out, Ned could see the moonlight reflecting off the spools of dust kicked up by the skidding horses.

The horsemen looked in the direction of the deputies' camp. Ned was sure of it, even though he could only see their dark silhouettes.

"Over there," one of the riders called out, and Ned saw him point with an out-thrust arm. "Them marshals are over there."

"Hush, Harvey. Not so loud," said another man.

The voices carried far on the still night air and Ned had no trouble hearing the words. And then he heard only the excited buzzing of hushed voices as the riders discussed something among themselves.

With a sickening feeling, Ned wondered if the one the riders called Harvey was the same big brute who had sat at the next table at the fish house when he and his men were questioning the cook about Gaton and Van Hook. He couldn't remember for sure, but he thought Madonna had said that the fisherman's name was Harvey. Yes, Harvey Cardin, he thought. That was the name the cook had mentioned.

It didn't really matter at this point. Ned knew he and his deputies were in trouble.

"Frank. Ted. Wake up," Remington whispered. "We got trouble."

"I'm awake," Shaw whispered back. "I woke up the same time you did. I hear 'em."

"Me, too," whispered Beck without moving.

"Stay put, but keep your weapons handy," Ned cautioned. "They may come after us, but if they head for the village, we'll go after them."

The three deputies moved only enough to snag their pistols and rifles from their resting places and to check their weapons. They turned and silently watched the group of riders who were still talking softly among themselves. Ned didn't have to say any more to his men. He had every confidence in them. They were experienced men and they were damned good at their job. When the time came, they'd do what they had to.

"Let's get 'em while they're asleep," called out the first voice.

"Shut up, Harvey," said another man in a loud, hushed voice. "Do you wanta wake 'em up, you damned fool?"

"I told you we'd find them marshals out here," said the voice that belonged to Harvey.

"You told us they were staying at the hotel," argued the other man. "We wasted a whole damned hour there checking them rooms."

"It don't matter," Harvey said. "Paco's gonna be so damned happy we killed 'em, he's gonna piss his pants."

"We ain't killed 'em yet, you dummy, so shut your mouth," said a deep, gravelly voice Ned hadn't heard before.

"Hell, I was the one who told Paco about them marshals bein' in town," Harvey said, "so you got no right to tell me to shut up."

"That don't make you special, Harvey," said the gravel voice.

"It does too," Harvey argued. "Paco promised to pay us a lot of money if we killed the marshals and that half-breed gal. If it weren't for me, none of you would be in on this."

"Hush! Both of you," said a fourth voice.

The hackles on the back of Remington's neck rose.

"Is Harvey the brute who was eating at the fish house?" he whispered.

"He must be," Beck said.

"I thought so," Remington said.

"Then the bastard told Gaton and his friends that we were in town asking questions," Shaw said in a low voice.

"It doesn't matter," Remington whispered. "Gaton is smart enough to know he's gonna have the law on his ass. Harvey just let him know we'd come this far. Gaton may be harder to find now that he knows we're here, but we'll track him down."

The three lawmen fell silent again and tried to make out the words of the distant horsemen.

"Let's go get 'em!" came the hushed battle cry.

Ned and his men watched and suddenly all five riders were headed their way at a fast gallop, their long rifles silhouetted.

"You ready?" Ned asked his men as he readied his rifle.

"Ready," said Beck.

"Ready," repeated Shaw.

"Then let's get those bastards," Remington said. "Before they get us."

Chapter Nine

Hoofbeats pounded the ground as the five horses barreled toward the lawmen's quiet camp. Grit and dust, kicked up by the fast-moving animals, hung in the air like a gray cloud in their wake.

Remington and his men were ready for the charging horsemen. Just after the bushwackers started in their direction, the three deputies had crawled across the ground on their bellies, rifles in hand, loaded pistols tucked into their belts. They had crawled from their bedrolls to the far end of the clump of trees behind them, away from the horses. They hadn't bothered to put on their boots or gunbelts.

Ned now stood next to a tree where his shape blended in with the dark foilage of the leaves. He had a good view of the charging bushwackers and was prepared to raise his rifle when the time was right. Shaw and Beck stood near other trees where they could watch the fast-approaching horsemen.

Ned glanced out at the bedrolls that were thirty feet away. The deputies' hats still sat on their respective saddles, each one near the head of a bedroll. Ned hoped the bushwackers would think that the lawmen were still asleep in the bedrolls, although he couldn't imagine anyone dumb enough to ride into a trap. If the riders had realized how far their voices had carried, they would use more caution than they seemed to be using, riding out in the open that way. Maybe they knew, and maybe they had a trick or two of their own to try on the lawmen.

Remington's muscles tautened as he watched the men looming up on them. His nerves felt like they were coiled tight, ready to spring. The rifle felt suddenly heavy in his hands. He held the butt of the weapon with one hand, his finger near the trigger. His other hand was cupped under the barrel, ready to raise it.

Ned didn't like the odds, five against three, but he knew that he and his men had the advantage. They knew where the attackers were and they could judge when and where to fire.

The seconds ticked by and the men seemed to come at them in slow motion. The closer they got, the bigger the men looked. Ned knew that Harvey was a big brute of a man. He tried to figure out which rider was Harvey, but all of the men seemed to be the same size. From what he could see, Ned figured Paco Gaton and Peter Van Hook had plenty of big brutes to call on when they needed someone to go out and remove the barriers that got in the way of their profitable, but illegal cattle rustling business.

Remington knew one thing. Paco Gaton and Norville Haskins weren't among the five bushwackers who were storming down on the lawmen's camp. Gaton was a short, small man and although Haskins was tall, Lina had said that he was lean and round-shouldered. None of the attackers could be considered lean.

Ned eased his finger around the trigger, and waited. He took a deep breath, let it out slowly. The riders were close enough now for Remington to see that they carried their rifles in one hand, pointed toward the ground, while they held the reins with the other hand. They were also close enough so that Ned would have no trouble picking off at least one of them. Still, he waited.

"Now!" shouted one of the riders when they were some twenty feet from the bedrolls. All five men instantly dropped the reins, brought their rifles up and fired into the bedrolls. The loud blasts exploded the stillness of the night. The horses, still in a forward motion, carried the riders closer to the blankets and the men fired again. The second round of explosions reverberated through the air.

The horses neighed and snorted and bumped into each other in the confusion.

Ned raised his rifle, took aim, and shot at the closest rider. The man's horse bucked just at that instant and Remington's shot caught the man in the lower leg.

The wounded man cried out in pain and dropped his weapon as he reached down for his leg. The rifle clattered to the ground and bounced onto one of the bedrolls.

"Oh, shit!" cried one of the other riders.

Frank Shaw and Ted Beck opened fire an instant after Ned had shot. In the mass of confused horses that were going one way and then another, both men missed their marks.

The wounded man grabbed up the loose reins that had fallen to his saddle. He jerked his frightened

horse around and high-tailed it for the road, still holding his leg, and still moaning in pain.

"They ain't there," one man called out. "Where are
they?"

"They're in the trees, Harvey, you dumbass!" another one shouted. "Shoot 'em!" The man whipped
out a pistol and fired blindly at the middle trees,
missing the lawmen at one end of the line of trees by
a good five feet, and missing the deputies' horses at
the other end by at least ten feet.

Remington drew his pistol out of the band of his
trousers and fired at Harvey before the fisherman
could get his own pistol out of its holster. Because
Harvey's horse was constantly changing directions in
the confusion, Ned knew when he fired that he didn't
have a clean shot. The bullet caught Harvey's hat and
sent it sailing in the air.

"Shit! I'm getting out of here!" Harvey cried. His
horse bucked and while he was struggling to find his
reins, Frank Shaw fired at him. Shaw missed him,
too. "Don't shoot! I'm leaving!" Harvey shouted. He
tossed his pistol to the ground as if to prove that he
was no threat to them. He snatched up the reins, and
headed for the road to join the other man who was
already riding toward the river front.

The three remaining bushwackers fired at the trees,
trying to pinpoint the obscure lawmen. They came
close a couple of times, but with Ned and his men
returning fire, the riders kept their horses on the
move.

One of the lawmen's bullets grazed the shooting
arm of a nearby rider.

"I've been hit!" the man cried. His hand fell open
and before the pistol tumbled from his grip, he

snatched it up with the other hand. "You bastards!" he shouted. He fired left-handed into the trees. When the misdirected bullet thudded into a high tree branch, the man gave up and headed for home, leaving a trail of dust behind him.

The two men who remained kept their distance as they rode around in circles and peered into the dark trees. They took aim a couple of times, but didn't fire.

"Come on, Jake. Let's get the hell out of here," one man said after a minute.

"But Paco said Van Hook wouldn't pay us unless we killed 'em," said the man with a bushy beard.

"To hell with both of them," said the first man. He took off as the others had done.

The bearded man looked back into the trees one more time and then followed his comrade.

Ned and his deputies waited in the trees until the bushwackers were well away from the camp before they emerged.

"I'm glad that's over with," Ned sighed as he walked over to the bedrolls. "We'd better check the horses to make sure they weren't hurt."

"I'll do it," Tom Beck offered. He sat down on his bedroll and tugged his boots on, then headed for the horses.

"It isn't over, Ned," Shaw said as he slipped into his own boots. "They'll be back."

"Not tonight." Ned reached down to his blankets and picked up the rifle that had fallen from the wounded man's hand. "Not a bad rifle. I've never seen fellows like that who tucked their tails between their legs and ran off like frightened pups. From the size of them, I thought they'd be pretty tough."

Shaw laughed. "I guess Van Hook figures big is brave."

Beck returned from the trees. "None of the horses were hit, but I think the exchange of gunfire scared the shit out of them. I just stepped in it." He glanced down at one of his boots, then walked away and scraped it back and forth across the damp grass.

"It scared the shit out of me," Ned laughed. "From what that one fellow said, I think Paco Gaton was the one who hired those fumbling idiots."

"I think so, too," said Beck as he checked his boot. "But Van Hook's footing the bill. He's the big man in this operation."

"That's what I figured," Ned said as he sat down on his blanket.

Frank Shaw strolled over and picked up the pistol Harvey Cardin had tossed to the ground. He handed it to Ned. "Here's another gun to add to your collection. So Harvey, the fisherman, turned out to be a rat."

"It looks that way," Remington said.

"I'm sure as hell glad we didn't stay at the hotel," Shaw said as he shook his head. "We'd have been trapped rats."

"I wonder where Paco Gaton and Norville Haskins are staying," Ned said. "It's obvious they aren't down in Texas where I thought they'd be."

"Why do you say that?" Beck asked.

"Because you said it was a day's ride to the Red River Station from here and Harvey wasn't gone that long. We saw him leave the fish house and go across the street to the saloon about two this afternoon. I figure it's close to four o'clock in the morning now."

"That's fourteen hours," Shaw said.

"Could he ride that far and back in that time?" Ned asked.

"No, he couldn't have ridden that far that fast," Beck said.

"Harvey's a fisherman, according to Madonna," Shaw said. "Maybe he went by boat."

"Not to the Red River Station. That would have take him a lot longer."

"Don't forget, Harvey and the others spent an hour searching the River Front Hotel for us," Shaw said. "You gotta figure that time in."

"That's right," said Remington. "I figure Harvey must be one of those friends of Gaton's Killbuck warned us about."

"I think so, too," Beck said.

"I think he was watching for us," Ned said, "and I think he would have spotted us anyway, but good ol' Harvey got damned lucky when we decided to have lunch at the fish house."

"He sure did," Shaw said, "but he had nothing to report to Gaton except that we were in town looking for him and that we'd probably be staying at the River Front Hotel."

"Do you suppose Harvey saw me talking to Killbuck out back of the restaurant?" Ned asked.

"No," said Beck. "I kept my eye on the saloon while you were gone, and he didn't come out."

"Do you think Gaton and Haskins are staying in town?" Ned asked.

"No," said Beck. "If they'd been staying at the River Front, Harvey could have gotten word to them in a hurry and they would have tailed us out to Killbuck's place."

"You're right."

"My guess is that Paco and his friend are staying in some little place near the river. I figure Harvey took his boat downstream and met them."

"Then we'll have to go looking for them," Ned said. "If they're hiding out, it might be hard to find them."

"I don't think so, and again, this is just a hunch," Beck said. "I think that when Harvey reports back to Gaton, which probably won't be until tomorrow morning, I think Gaton and Haskins will high-tail it down to Van Hook's ranch to tell him. If we're lucky, we'll find all three men at Van Hook's."

"I hope you're right, Frank," Ned said with a sigh. "It would be nice to arrest all of them in one swoop of the handcuffs."

· "I'm sure it won't be quite that easy, Ned," Shaw laughed. "We gotta earn our money, don't we?"

Shaw plopped down on his blankets and started to remove his boots. "Don't you think we should get some sleep before dawn?" he said with a big yawn.

Ned looked at the star-studded sky. "Hell, it's almost dawn now. By the time we get our gear stowed away, it'll be time to head for Killbuck's place."

"Aw, shucks," Shaw said.

"I'll tell you one thing," Remington said as he put his boots on. "After tonight, I'm definitely not going to take Lina Miller with us."

"Would you care to place a little bet on that?" Beck said.

Chapter Ten

Charlie Killbuck was already in the shed, saddling his Indian pony by lamplight, when the three deputies arrived shortly before dawn.

"I am glad you are here," Killbuck said when he saw them. "I heard gunfire a while ago and I thought maybe someone had ambushed you as you rode out here from town."

"We didn't stay in town, Charlie," Ned said.

"You didn't? I thought you were going to stay at the hotel."

"We changed our minds. But there was trouble," Ned said. "Some of Gaton's friends found us where we were camped out."

"You were not hurt, were you?" Killbuck looked at each man.

"No," said Ned as he eased out of the saddle.

"Did you kill these men?"

"No. We nicked a couple of them, but they ran off scared before we could do much damage."

"I am glad you are safe, but the men will try again." Killbuck shook his head. "If not those men, then others will try to kill you."

"We know," Ned said. "That's why it's important

for Lina to go back to Galena with Tom Beck this
morning. It's just too dangerous for her to ride with
us."

"Lina is in the house getting ready to ride with us,"
Killbuck said. "She asked me to saddle up her pony."

"She can't go," Ned insisted.

"Yes, I can," said Lina as she came into the shed.
"I'm all ready."

Ned whirled around to face the girl and as he did,
he caught the delicate scent of her perfume. She carried heavy saddlebags over her shoulder and wore
boys' clothing: a fresh brown shirt, clean, dark
trousers and polished boots. Her long, dark hair was
tucked up under the same black, wide-brimmed hat
she'd worn the day before. She had added a brown
scarf to her clothing and tied it around her neck. Ned
wondered if she had done that because he was wearing a brown scarf around his neck.

"Lina, it's just too dangerous," Ned told her.
"Some of Gaton's friends found us earlier this morning. And they came after us with guns blazing. Can't
you understand how dangerous this is?"

"You survived, didn't you? Well, so can I," she
said smugly. "And don't be too damned surprised if I
end up saving your butt."

Ned was surprised by her language, but realized
that the girl was doing everything she could to go
along with them.

"Lina, please listen to me," Ned said.

"I'm going to Texas with you," she said in her
stubborn way. "And if you won't take me, I'll just
follow you anyway."

Remington stared down at the dirt floor and kicked
at the hard ground with the toe of his boot.

"All right, Lina, you can go with us, but I can no longer be responsible for your safety."

Lina smiled. "I can take care of myself," she said, "and I can shoot my way out of any mess you get us into."

Ned resented her smug attitude, but he didn't say anything. He knew the girl couldn't possibly realize what kind of dangers they would face. He hoped she could shoot as well as she said she could.

"You'll do as your told without question," he told her harshly. "And you'll follow all of my rules."

"What rules?" she asked.

"For one, you won't wear any damned perfume on this trip," he said, "and I'll think of the other rules as we go."

"You don't have any rules, Remington," she giggled. She slid the heavy saddlebags off her shoulder and handed them to her uncle.

"You aren't taking your whole wardrobe with you, are you, Miss Miller?" Ned said as he nodded to her saddlebags. "We have to travel light and all you need is one change of clothes."

"That's all I'm taking, Mr. Remington. Besides a few necessities I'm taking along, the rest of the contents of my saddlebags is food for the trip. There are several tins of food that won't spoil in the heat, and I brought along some smoked fish and venison, and dried veal. I took the liberty of making a few sandwiches for all of us and I baked some cookies and pastries."

"This isn't a picnic, Miss Miller." Ned hated himself for being so sarcastic when he actually appreciated what she had done.

"I'm well aware of that, Mr. Remington." Lina

stared at him with her deep blue eyes. "And if we're going to be riding together, I think we should be on a first-name basis. May I call you Ned?"

Remington smiled. "Yes, Lina, you may call me Ned. And if everybody's ready, we'd better get going."

"Do we have to ride through town?" Frank Shaw asked.

"No," said Charlie Killbuck. "We will cut across the fields and go west for a couple of miles before we turn south to get to the narrow part of the river where we will cross it."

"Good," said Ned as he watched Lina slide up onto her saddle. He noticed that she was quite comfortable with her spotted pony.

Lina rode out of the shed first and waited for the others.

"Go ahead," Killbuck told the deputies as he walked over to the lantern. He turned the wick down until it flickered and sputtered, and waited until the flame died out completely. Then he mounted his pony and followed the marshals out of the shed. The gray sky was already beginning to lighten in the east.

Killbuck led the way, with Lina right behind him. Once they were beyond his pasture and into a more wooded section of the land, Ned never saw the river front town again.

When they got to the narrow part of the river two hours later, Killbuck told them they would stop long enough to water their horses before they crossed.

Lina slid down easily from her mount. She led her horse down to the edge of the water and let him drink his fill. The others watered their horses and when they went back up the bank, Lina was sitting on the ground removing her boots.

"Better take your boots off unless you want to spend the rest of the day in squishy boots," she said. "Everything else will dry out quick enough in the heat of the day." She stood up and tucked her boots under the thongs that held her bedroll in place behind her saddle.

Ned glanced at the two deputies, shrugged his shoulders, then sat on the ground and took his boots off. The others did the same.

"You men probably didn't have breakfast this morning," Lina said after all of the boots were securely in place. "Would you like a pastry?"

"No thanks," Ned said, "I'm not hungry. But I want to fill my canteen before we ford the river."

Killbuck and Lina waited on their horses while the three deputies filled their canteens. When they were ready to go, Charlie led the way. They all held their weapons high in the air as the horses walked out into the chilly river. When the water was chest high on the animals, they began to swim. A few minutes later, the horses sogged up on the bank on the other side of the river.

Water dripped from the riders' socks and pantlegs as they emerged from the river and Ned was glad that he had removed his boots. His socks would dry soon enough and then he could put his boots back on. He now had a little more respect for Lina Miller.

Charlie Killbuck led them across an uninhabited stretch of land and except to stop to rest their horses every hour, they pushed on at a steady pace. They put their boots back on about ten o'clock, when their socks were finally dry. They never saw another person as they rode and about noon they stopped long enough to eat some of the sandwiches Lina had fixed.

Ned was glad that Lina had brought the food and he told her so. After the men were through eating the sandwiches, Lina offered them cookies and pastries. Not wanting to ride on a full stomach, the men took only one cookie apiece and washed it down with water from their canteens.

They pushed on and it was nearly six o'clock in the late afternoon when they finally spotted the main body of the Red River, which they would have to cross to get to the Red River Station. Still, they had not seen another person.

"I think we should bed down here for the night," Charlie Killbuck said. "We do not want to cross the river after dark. The Red River Station is a busy place and we do not know what awaits us over there."

"Yes," Ned agreed. "It will be better to arrive in full daylight, when we are well-rested."

Charlie Killbuck led them to a thick stand of cottonwoods and found a place where they could spread their bedrolls out among the trees. There was a small stream nearby that fed into the Red River. They took care of their horses first and tied them up for the night. Ned insisted that there be no fire built that night and after the blankets were in place, Lina brought out the food from her saddlebags.

They ate the rest of the sandwiches, which Lina insisted wouldn't last another day, and shared a tin of peaches. They snacked on smoked fish and raw carrots from Killbuck's garden. When they were through, Lina brought out the sweets. This time, they each took a rich pastry, and two of the cookies that were beginning to crumble in their tin.

It was dark by the time they finished eating. The stars seemed closer than they had the night before and Ned could see the glow of the low, rising moon, through the trees.

"You're a good cook, Lina," Ned said as he stood up. "Thanks for bringing this food along."

"Yes," said Tom Beck. "We were getting a little tired of hardtack and beans."

"Goodness, is that all you men have been eating?" Lina said as she took her hat off and let her long hair tumble free. She started to clear away the mess from the meal.

"It seems like it," Frank Shaw laughed. "But your food was delicious, Lina."

"Lina is a good girl, except for her stubborn streak," Killbuck said proudly. "And she is a good cook, but I ate too much." He patted his stomach. "It is a good thing we will not ride tonight."

"I'm glad you all liked it, and there's plenty more for tomorrow," Lina said.

"You'll spoil us," Ned said.

"You deserve it," Lina said. "It must be hard being a marshall when you have to be out on the trail so much and you have to carry all your food and your whole kitchen with you."

"Our whole kitchen?" Shaw asked.

"I mean your utensils and pots and pans."

"It isn't so bad," Beck said. "We can pick up supplies when we pass through the towns."

"Just wait till you sleep on the hard ground tonight," Shaw said. "Then you'll know how much fun being a marshal is."

"I'm looking forward to sleeping out under the stars," she said. "Ned, would you mind walking down to the stream with me so I can fill my canteen?"

"You aren't afraid of the dark, are you?" he teased.

"It's a little scary out there," she said as she peered out at the dark, shadowy trees.

The girl was being honest and Ned resisted the urge to say something sarcastic. "Sure, I want to fill my canteen, too. Anybody else?"

"As long as you're going that way," Tom Beck said as he handed Ned his canteen.

"Mine, too," said Shaw. "I don't think I can move another muscle."

"I'll take yours, Uncle Charlie," Lina said.

Canteens in hand, Ned and Lina walked toward the stream, ducking around low branches.

"It's brighter out here than I thought it would be," Lina said as they neared the water.

"We're out away from the dense trees," Ned said. "It's a bright, starlit night out and the water reflects the starlight."

Lina looked up at the stars, then down at the water. "I see that now."

"The moon's coming up over there and when it's a little higher, it'll be even brighter."

"Good, it isn't so scary."

Just as they reached the stream bank, an owl hooted from a nearby tree. Lina gasped and reached for Ned's arm.

"It was only an owl, Lina."

"I guess I'm not as brave as I thought I was," she said with a self-conscious giggle. She quickly let go of his arm.

"I reckon I wasn't either the first time I spent the night outside," Ned said as he began to fill the first of the canteens. "You'll get used to the night noises, and if you're smart, you'll learn to recognize them."

"Is that what you do?" Lina dipped her canteen into the edge of the water.

"Yes. I listen very carefully to all of the sounds. That way, I can tell when I hear a noise that shouldn't be there."

"That's a good idea," Lina said.

"It's a necessity in my line of work. But, it's really no different from sleeping in a house. You get used to the house creaking and settling. You hear the clock chime. You hear the cat or dog roaming around the house. You expect the tree branches to brush across your windows when it's windy. These things don't scare you because you're accustomed to them. But let a strange noise creep in and I'll bet you hide your head under the covers."

"You're right," Lina said. "From now on I'll pay more attention to what's around me."

"It could save your life."

"I guess you and your men are plenty smart about such things."

"We've learned from experience. As lawmen, we have to stay one jump ahead of the criminals we're tracking, or we're dead meat."

Lina looked over at him as she withdrew the canteen from the water. "That's a terrible way to put it."

"But it's true," Ned said. "And since you insisted on coming along on this trip, I want you to learn as much as possible. The time may come when you won't get a chance to use your expertise with a pistol unless you're smarter than the other fellow."

"What else should I know?"

"Being aware of your surroundings is probably the most important thing," Ned said as he filled the third canteen. "Look over your shoulder and watch your backtrail. Scan the countryside and watch for places where you can take cover if you need to. Watch for distant spools of dust that would indicate a wagon or a rider. Smell the air and learn to recognize the different odors. Watch the weather so you don't get caught out in a bad storm."

"That's a lot to learn in a short time."

"You can train yourself to be observant. It'll become second nature to you." Ned pulled the canteen from the water and stuffed the cork in it. "Another thing. Always keep your horse at an even pace except for the times when you need a short burst of speed. And stop to rest him once in a while. If you push your pony too hard and get him lathered, he's likely to drop dead on you. And without your horse, you're . . ."

"Dead meat," Lina laughed.

"You're learning. Are you ready to head back to camp?"

"Yes." When Lina stood up, the owl screeched again. Lina let out a little cry. "I guess it'll take time," she laughed.

"And that's something we don't have much of, so you'd better sleep on it. I'm counting on finding Paco Gaton and the others tomorrow."

"It's going to be dangerous, isn't it?" she said.

Lina looked up at him and he saw the fear reflected in her bright blue eyes.

"I'm afraid so, Lina," he said. "It'll probably be the most dangerous thing you'll ever have to face in your life."

Chapter Eleven

"I thought you were just trying to scare me back at the house so I wouldn't tag along," Lina said as they started back toward the camp.

"I told it straight, Lina," Ned said.

"I realize that now. I guess I figured that since you and your men were deputy marshals, you could just march up to the outlaws and arrest them, by virtue of your authority. But I know now that even if you find them, those brutal criminals aren't going to give up without a fight."

"It's not too late for Tom Beck to take you back to Galena," Ned said. "You can start back tomorrow morning."

"No, that would make you a man short, and I think you're going to need all the help you can get. I've come this far and I'll see it through."

"Just promise me that you won't let your hatred of these men cause you to do something stupid," Ned said. "I don't want you rushing in and trying to kill them if you see them, no matter how you feel about them. You wouldn't stand a chance."

"I'd be dead meat," Lina laughed.

But there was a nervousness to her laughter this

time that had not been there before, and Ned noticed her shudder with a chill that coursed through her body. Maybe that was a good sign. Maybe she really was beginning to realize how dangerous this case was. And if she had a healthy respect for her own safety, that would be a big asset to all of them.

"Just be careful, Lina," he said. "We'll protect you all we can, but if it comes to a showdown, you may have to fend for yourself."

"I don't want you to be worrying about me when you've got more important things to do," she said. "I can handle a gun if I have to, and I promise I'll be careful."

"Good girl." Ned patted her on the head as if she were a puppy who'd just mastered her first trick.

"Are you married, Ned?" Lina asked as they neared the camp.

"I was. Does it matter?"

"No. I just thought that if you were married, your wife must be terribly worried about you when you're gone like this. Is that why you're not together anymore?"

Ned didn't want to talk about it and he knew it would serve no purpose to explain his situation. "She died about three years ago."

"Oh, I'm sorry," Lina said. "Do you have any children?"

"One daughter. A little older than you."

"Where is she?"

"Back in Galena."

"Does she worry about you when you're gone?" Lina looked over at Ned. "I would if you were my father."

"Katy's learned to live with it."

"Katy. That's a pretty name. I'll bet she's proud of you."

"I wouldn't know about that," Ned said, relieved that they were back at the camp. "We're back with full canteens," he announced.

Frank Shaw was already asleep and snoring gently. Charlie Killbuck and Tom Beck were sitting on their blankets, talking.

"Good," said Charlie. "We're ready to turn in for the night."

"So early?" Lina said as she handed one of the canteens to her uncle.

"Lina, these men are tired," Charlie said. "They got very little sleep last night and they face a busy day tomorrow."

"I know," Lina said.

"Rule number two, Lina," Ned said. "We go to bed with the chickens and get up before dawn."

Lina crinkled up her nose and gave him a funny look. "I'll go to bed, but I can't promise you I'll go right to sleep. I'm just not sleepy yet."

"Then stay awake and think about the things I told you," Ned said. "Goodnight, everybody."

Ned was surprised that it was already getting light out when he awoke the following morning. Usually he was up long before dawn. He must have been more tired than he'd realized because he'd fallen asleep almost as soon as his head hit the coat pillow. It was the best night's sleep he'd had since they left home and it would probably be the only decent sleep he would get until they returned to Galena.

He sat up and yawned, wiped the sleep from his eyes. He flexed muscles that were stiff from sleeping

on the hard ground, then rolled his head around and
rubbed the back of his neck.

He looked over at Lina's bedroll, and saw that she
was still asleep. When he glanced at the other bedrolls, he got a start. All of the men were gone. Frank,
Tom and Charlie Killbuck. He cocked his head and
heard their muffled voices way off in the trees. He
heard the crunching of leaves and knew they were
returning from their morning rituals.

Fully awake, he slipped into his boots, then
jumped up and wandered off into the woods to relieve
himself. When he got back, Lina was gone and the
men were busy saddling the horses and stowing the
gear.

"Good morning, Ned," Frank Shaw said. "You
sawed the logs last night."

"Good morning, gentlemen," Ned said. "I feel
rested this morning. How about you?"

"We feel good, Ned," Shaw said.

"Yes," said Beck. "It was very quiet here last
night."

"I told you we would not see anyone," Killbuck
said with a satisfied smile. He tossed Lina's saddlebags up behind her saddle and fastened the leather
strap that held the leather pouches in place. His own
horse was already saddled and ready to ride.

"You're a good guide, Charlie." Ned glanced at the
eastern sky and saw the flare of pink through the foilage. The sun would be up before they could get
away. Even though it would be warm that day, Ned
slipped his buckskin jacket on and checked the big,
inside pocket to make sure the three warrants were
still there. He did it out of habit.

"Thank you, Ned," Killbuck said. "I hope our luck is as good today."

"It will be. I can feel it in my bones." Ned carried his saddle over to his Missouri trotter and slung it up over the saddle blanket that was already draped over the horse's back. "That a boy, Neal," he said, and stroked the sleek, black hide of the big trotter's neck. He cinched the saddle down, checked it, then went back for his saddlebags.

"I think it's going to be a little cooler today," Beck said. He climbed up in his saddle, patted his restless horse's neck.

"Yes," said Killbuck. He stood between his pony and Lina's, clutching the ropes of both reins in his hand. Lina's wide-brimmed hat sat on top of her saddle. "There are a few clouds in the sky, but not enough to bring the rain we need."

"You and Lina can turn back if you want to," Ned said as he secured his saddlebags behind his saddle. "I'm sure we can find the ferry from here if you point us in the right direction."

"We will go with you," Killbuck said.

"I don't want either one of you to risk your life," Ned said. "My boys and I are getting paid to put our lives on the line. You're not."

Killbuck's face got as dark as a cloud. "It was my brother and Lina's father who were murdered," he said with tight lips that reminded Ned of Lina's stubborn pout. "I will be happy to give up my life if it will help bring those bastards to court. I know they will hang for their crimes."

"I know they will, too," Ned said somberly. He felt the weight of responsibility suddenly heavy on his shoulders. So many people were counting on him to bring those three outlaws to justice. Judge Barnstall, Lina, Charlie Killbuck, the people of the Cherokee village, the people who had been victims of Van Hook's cattle rustling ring. And just as important, the people who would become victims if the ring of violent rustlers wasn't stopped.

He shook out his bedroll out. Harder than he had planned to, but it helped to vent some of his frustration. He was rolling the blankets up when Lina walked back into the camp. She came from the direction of the stream. Her long, dark hair was damp and Ned saw that she had scrubbed her face. She wore a clean, light brown shirt, creased from being in her saddlebags. The dark brown trousers and scarf were the same ones she'd worn the day before.

"We are all ready to go, Lina," Killbuck said.

Ned carried his bedroll over to his horse and strapped it on top of his saddlebags.

"But I was planning to fix breakfast for you before we leave," Lina said.

"No, Lina," Killbuck said. "The sun is already coming up and we still have an hour's ride to the ferry."

"But you could eat some fruit and pastries," the girl said. "That wouldn't take long."

"No," said Charlie. "It will be safer for us to cross the river early in the morning, when many people are still asleep." He reached up and got her hat off her saddle, held it out for her.

"You're right, Uncle Charlie." Lina piled her hair on top of her head, then took the hat from her uncle and stuffed it on her head, trapping the damp, dark locks beneath it. She took the reins from Killbuck, slid her boot into the stirrup, and pulled herself up on the saddle.

The five riders left the camp site as clean as they found it. Lina carried the crumpled wrappings from the sandwiches in her saddlebags. They rode toward the southwest and although the rising sun wasn't directly behind them, they didn't have to ride into the low sun and be blinded by its light.

Ned saw the massive expanse of the Red River in the far distance long before he saw any signs of civilization. They were on a hilltop when he first spotted it and the way the sun's light reflected off of the water, the river looked like a long golden ribbon that had been casually dropped on a carpet of green velvet. He supposed that sometimes the river actually took on a red hue, at sunset or dawn, if the skies billowed with clouds that were tinged with the right shades of red.

As they got closer to the river, small adobe huts and wooden shacks began to dot the land. Most of them looked abandoned.

Just as Charlie Killbuck had said, an hour after they left their camp, Ned and his group arrived at the quiet river town where they would ferry across to the Red River Station. A large wooden sign at the entrance to the small, tree-lined village displayed the name of the town in neatly carved letters. Appropriately enough, the town was called Riverside.

When Killbuck reined up and paused for a moment, Remington fished his gold watch out of his pocket and checked the time. It was almost seven in the morning and he could see, when he glanced at the main part of town to his left, that there weren't many people stirring this early. The few men he saw on the boardwalks looked like businessmen who were getting ready to start another day.

The town seemed quieter, more peaceful than the other river front town near Tishomingo. Maybe it was the early hour that made it seem that way. Perhaps the town would be a bustle of activity by noon. The odor of decaying fish was just as strong as it had been in Tishomingo, but this town seemed cleaner, more respectable, than the other one.

Killbuck didn't take them to the business part of the town. Instead he turned right and led them to a pretty stretch of land on the high river bank which was obviously a place where people came to sit in the shade for a while and gaze out at the river and see Texas on the other side, or watch the passing boats, or just sit and relax.

There were more than a dozen wooden benches in the tranquil setting. Most of them were located near trees that would offer shade from the hot, mid-day sun. A couple of the benches sat out in the open where a person could sit and sun himself on a chilly afternoon.

No one was there this time of morning, but Ned could picture small groups of little old men sitting on the benches, their small hats shading their failing eyes from the sun as they whittled chunks of wood with withered, vein-lined hands, just like the old men back in Galene did in the town square. He could imagine a young, long-skirted mother sitting on a bench, rocking the baby in the carriage as she stared out at the river, and thought about faraway places. He could see elderly couples talking about old times as they tossed scraps of food to the birds.

It was a place where Ned would like to sit and

relax for a spell without the pressures that were on him now.

"Come on, let's have a closer look," Charlie said. He dismounted, looped his reins over the hitchrail, and walked in among the empty benches. Ned and the others tied their horses to the rail and followed him. "There it is," he said, pointing down the bank toward the docks.

"There's what? Texas?" Shaw asked in his slow drawl as he ambled up behind Charlie, limping slightly, as he always did.

"No, Texas is across the river," Killbuck said. "Down there. There's the ferry we'll be taking across the river."

The other four people stretched their necks to look down.

Ned saw the flat raft with its high, wooden plank sides. There was a shorter railing across the front of the ferry and only a rope stretched across the back. The ferry was twice as big as the one in Tishomingo and on one side, near the back, there was a tiny, enclosed cubicle with windows all around. There was a man in there now and Ned figured that's where the crew kept their paperwork. And he thought the men who worked on the ferry probably used the enclosure when the weather was cold or wet.

A few feet from the ferry, a big ship rocked in the water. It was tied to the dock with two heavy ropes and five or six dock workers were already loading crates onto the ship in the early morning coolness.

"The ferry looks like it's big enough to hold all of us," Ned said.

"Yes, it will hold at least ten horses and ten passengers," Killbuck said. "You people wait here where no one will see you while I go down and arrange our passage. It will be safer that way."

Killbuck mounted his horse and rode back to the path that led down to the dock. Ned and the others watched as Charlie got off his horse, walked aboard the ferry and talked to the man in the cubicle. Charlie held up five fingers, shook his head once, and nodded several times.

Within minutes, Charlie was back. He stayed on his horse. "Ross will take us across the river as soon as his partner gets back from eating breakfast at the cafe," he told the others. "The partner's name is Billy. Ross said that by the time we got loaded aboard, he would be ready to leave."

"Good," said Ned as he and the others headed for their horses. "We should be at the Red River Station within the hour."

"Yes," said Killbuck. "The ferry trip takes about thirty minutes. The total fare will two fifty. Twenty-five cents for each of us and twenty-five cents for each horse."

"Good enough," Remington said. "I'll pay for all of us."

Five minutes later, Ned and his group were on board the ferry and Ned had paid the fare. Ross, a pleasant fellow with dark, thinning hair, gray around the temples, waited at the back of the boat. A few minutes later, his younger partner, Billy, showed up. After the two men talked briefly, Ross moved to one side of the boat and stood beside a thick, mounted oar.

Billy, a muscular lad of about twenty, untied both ropes from the dock, then stepped onto the deck of the ferry. He walked to the opposite side of the boat, near Remington, and nodded to his partner that he was ready. Both men started rowing and the ferry slid through the water at a good clip once they got going.

They were nearly half way across the river before Billy turned and spoke to Ned.

"Nice time of day to be crossing," he said. "It gets awful hot in the afternoon."

"I can imagine. It's kind of chilly now." Ned pulled his buckskin coat closer around him and was glad that he was wearing it.

"I see you're a marshal," Billy said as he looked at Ned's badge.

"Yes," Ned said.

Billy's oar sliced into the water and he tugged hard on it. He had a puzzled look on his face. "Say, are those other fellows marshals?" He nodded toward the other passengers.

"Two of them are."

"I wonder if you're the three deputies them fellows were talking about last night."

Ned looked at Billy, a puzzled look on his face. "What fellows?"

"Two fellows I took across on the ferry late yesterday afternoon," Billy said. "One of them was a short Mexican and his name was Paco. I didn't ever hear the other man's name mentioned. They weren't very friendly, but I couldn't help but hear part of their conversation."

Ned frowned. "What'd they say?"

"Something about a fellow named Harvey. They said he'd messed up good. The Mexican said it didn't matter. He'd arrange to have a welcoming party waiting for the three deputies when they arrived on the other side of the river. Didn't make much sense to me."

"Damn. It does to me, Billy," Ned said. "We're looking for those two men. I've got warrants for their arrests right here in my pocket."

"Then why would they have a party for you if they know you're coming after them?" Billy asked.

"The party they're planning for us is going to be complete with gunfire."

Billy's eyes went wide. "You mean they're going to ambush you?"

"That's what I mean, Billy."

Chapter Twelve

"Jeeez, I'm sorry," said the young ferryman. "I didn't mean to worry you."

"I'm glad you told me, Billy," Remington said. "I hate surprise parties."

"Do you want us to turn the ferry around so you and your friends can go back to Riverside?" Billy stopped rowing briefly, but tugged on the oar again when the ferry started to go off course.

"Nope. We came here to arrest those bastards and that's what we're going to do. Knowing that they're planning to ambush us gives us the advantage."

"That's pretty dangerous, isn't it?" Billy asked. "Riding straight into an ambush?"

Ned saw the boy shudder. "Yes, it is. Do you know if Paco and his friend are going to be there?"

"I don't think so," Billy said. "They said something about rounding up five or six of the best men they had to wait for you. And then Paco and his partner were planning to ride to the Van Hook ranch near Nocona."

"Nocona? Where's that?"

"Almost straight west of the Red River Station. About ten miles."

115

"Do you know Van Hook?" Ned asked.

"No, but I've heard a lot about the man." Billy shook his head. "All bad. I guess he's got a lot of money. He runs stolen cattle, I think."

"He does."

"Paco mentioned something about finding a half-breed girl. Can't remember her name. Linda or Leeanne. Something like that. I guess she must be at the Red River Station, or maybe at Van Hook's ranch. It didn't make any sense to me."

Ned glanced at Lina. She was standing at the front of the boat with the other three men, watching the ferry cut through the water, occasionally glancing at the Texas shoreline. He was glad that she was dressed like a boy. The hired gunmen would be watching for three marshals and maybe they wouldn't figure that Lina and her uncle were part of the same group.

Remington fished a five-dollar bill out of his pocket and handed it to the boy. "Have a beer on me, Billy. You deserve it."

Billy's eyes got wide. He let his oar drag, then quickly put it back in motion when he realized it. He hesitated a minute before he finally took the money from Ned.

"Well, thank you, sir," the boy grinned. "But you didn't have to do that. I didn't like Paco and his friend and I would have told you anything I knew about them for nothing."

"I know you would have, Billy. You look like a decent chap."

"Thank you, sir," he said again.

"I've got to tell my friends what we're facing when we reach land."

"We'll put in at the dock in about five minutes,"

Billy said as he glanced out at the Texas shore. "But I don't think the gunmen will be waiting there for you. There'll be too many people around this time of a morning for them to open fire on the law."

"Where would they wait?"

Billy thought about it for a minute. "Probably up the bank, close to the Red River Station. They'd figure that's where you were going. There's high land just beyond the Station and if you can get up over that hill and out of sight, I think you stand a good chance of making it."

"Thanks," Ned said as he started for the front of the ferry.

"If I can remember anything else, I'll let you know."

Ned turned back and nodded, then continued toward his friends. "We got trouble waiting for us when we set foot on Texas soil," he said.

Tom Beck frowned. "What kind of trouble?"

"An ambush."

"Gaton and Haskins?" Frank Shaw asked.

"No. Hired guns," Ned said. He explained what Billy had told him.

Charlie Killbuck had a worried look on his face. Lina stood wide-eyed, listening to Remington's every word.

"And we're going to ride right into their nest?" Beck asked when Ned was through explaining.

"Yes," said Ned. "They plan to catch us by surprise, but we'll be the ones to surprise them. We'll be prepared."

"Why don't we turn around and head back for the other shore?" Frank asked. "We can find another way to get to Gaton and Haskins."

"We're not running away from trouble, Frank," Ned said. "We're gonna face it square in the eyes."

"How can you prepare for something like this?" Beck asked.

"By having our weapons ready when we ride off the ferry," Ned said as he studied the Texas shoreline that was getting closer all the time. "By watching for the ambushers. By finding the hired guns before they find us."

"Got any idea what these fellows look like?" Shaw asked.

"Probably much like the brutes who attacked us in Tishomingo," Ned laughed.

"I can help you," Killbuck said. "I know this land. I know the places where the gunmen could hide to wait for us. And I know where to go to get away from them."

"Charley, I wish you and Lina would stay on the ferry until this is over with," Ned said. "We're facing hired gunnies and they're expecting three lawmen to ride off this ferry. They probably don't even know about you and Lina. You'll both be safe here."

"I know I can be of help to you," Charlie said. "I will ride with you."

"Me, too," said Lina. "If you're outnumbered, you may need an extra gun on your side."

"Lina, please stay here on the ferry," Ned pleaded when he saw that they were quickly approaching the dock. He scanned the area around the dock and didn't see anyone who looked suspicious. But like Billy had said, the dock would be busy this time of morning and any one of the men he saw who looked like workers could actually be one of the gunnies.

"No," Lina said in her usual stubborn manner.

Ned felt the ferry swing around. He glanced back and saw that Billy and Ross were manuevering the boat around so that they would land with the loading end of the ferry near the dock. Ned and the others remained at the end of the ferry that was now farthest from the dock, but they turned around so they could keep an eye on the dock and the hill above it where the building of the Red River Station was located.

"Please, Lina," Ned said. "Billy will take care of you. We'll come back for you as soon as it's safe to do so."

"You know I won't stay here," Lina said. "We're in this together."

"We're docking now, sir," Billy called out from behind him.

"Thanks, Billy," Ned called back without turning around. "All right, Lina. You'll go with us. We'll all mount up and ride off the ferry instead of walking our horses off. You men scatter out as soon as we clear the dock area. Ride fast with your guns drawn. Keep your eyes open and if you see anyone fixin' to shoot at you, fire at them first and then get the hell out of here. Lina, you ride right behind me. The gunnies will be aiming at me and if I miss my shot, maybe you can pick him off."

The ferry bounced against dock. The passengers shifted weight to keep their balance.

While Ross stayed at his station and steadied the boat by twisting his oar around in the water, Billy hopped onto the wooden dock. The boy carried the two heavy ropes with him and quickly lashed them around the landing pegs that were mounted on the dock. He snugged the ropes tight, brought the ferry as close to the dock as he could. Then he stepped back onto the ferry and removed the waist-high rope barrier that stretched across the loading end of the vessel.

"We've landed, sir," he announced. He gestured with his arm, indicating that the passengers could disembark.

"Take your time mounting your horses," Ned told the others. "Ride off the ferry slowly, one at a time. I'll take the lead, with Lina right behind me. Act as normal as possible until we've cleared the dock. Then scatter and ride fast. But keep your eyes open in case the hired guns have positioned themselves among the dock workers."

Ned had been the last one to board the ferry, so his horse was already first in line to disembark. Using the reins, he pulled Neal around to face the dock, then eased himself up in the saddle and waited until the others were mounted.

Killbuck helped Lina turn her pony around and lined it up behind Ned. As Lina climbed up in the saddle, Killbuck tugged his own horse back so that he would be the last to disembark.

Tom Beck mounted his horse and reined it into line behind Lina. Frank Shaw stayed behind Beck.

Remington glanced back over his shoulder and saw that everyone was saddled up. All of them held their respective reins in their left hands. Their right hands were within easy reach of their holstered pistols.

He took a deep breath and felt his stomach whirl. His hands didn't tremble, but he knew that every muscle in his body was taut.

"Ready?" he said.

The four people behind him nodded in unison.

Chapter Thirteen

Remington sat tall in the saddle as he rode across the planks of the dock. He glanced around, as any other ferry rider would do after crossing into Texas. A few of the dock workers paused to look at the newcomers, but most of the muscular men were too busy hoisting heavy crates into waiting boats to bother with such an ordinary occurrence.

As he rode slowly up the narrow path that led to the top of the river bank and the town of Red River Station, Ned saw that there were plenty of places where the gunmen could be hiding. The main building of the docking station, off to the right, was actually painted red. Just beyond the station, he could see the pole fence of the stockyard and the few cattle that were near the fence. From his vantage point, he could see only a few more buildings of the town. The thick rows of trees blocked his view of everything else, except the high ground just beyond the station house, directly ahead of him.

The gunmen could be anywhere up there and Ned knew that his own men couldn't scatter out until they reached the open ground beyond the trees.

He drew his pistol just before he reached the rows

of trees on either side of the main road, and knew that the others would do the same. He thumbed back the hammer and snapped the reins, urging his horse to a full gallop. He raced by the trees and quickly looked in both directions. The gunmen weren't there where he'd expected them to be.

He rode straight ahead, toward the high ground, and again glanced in both directions as he passed the main street of the town. He saw only the townspeople who were minding their own business. As he neared the red station building on his right, Ned scanned the tree-dotted hill off to his left.

He was still studying the confusing pattern of gullies and ruts on the tree-dotted hill when four riders suddenly darted out from behind the red station building, riding straight for the deputies, guns blazing wildly.

Ned took quick aim and tumbled one rider out of his saddle with the first shot. Just before the ambusher hit the ground, Ned saw the blood gush from his chest and knew the wound was fatal.

Ned was beyond the station house now and out in the open. He knew his own men had scattered. Two of the gunmen suddenly changed directions and circled to Ned's left. The other one swung around to his right.

Tom Beck had gone to the left. He ducked a shot coming his way, then rose back up and fired at the men barreling down on him. His bullet crashed into the gunman's shoulder with a sickening thud. The shot wasn't a fatal one, but it was enough to stop the man and send him riding off toward the top of the hill. He wouldn't be back. It would be a long, long time before he could use his shooting arm.

The other two men zeroed in on Remington, one coming at him from each side, pistols aimed.

Beck and Killbuck shot simultaneously at the man on the left, but both were too far away to hit their mark. The gunman whirled around in his saddle and aimed at Killbuck. Ned fired before the gunman could get his shot off.

Ned's quick shot was low. It hit the man in the upper thigh. The gunman screamed out in pain as blood spurted through the hole in his leg and stained his trousers. The man whirled his horse around, dug spurs into his horse's side and took off up the hill.

Frank Shaw, who was closer to the wounded rider, took careful aim and fired. The gunman gasped as the bullet caught him in the lungs. He leaned to the left and slid out of his saddle, crumpled to the ground, pink foam gushing from his mouth. He wasn't dead when he hit the ground, but with his lungs exploded, he wouldn't take another breath.

Remington swung around in the saddle but couldn't get a shot off fast enough to stop the man who was coming straight at him from his right. The gunman's pistol was aimed between Ned's eyes. A shot rang and for a brief instant, Ned thought he'd been shot. He froze and waited for the bullet to plunge into his heart. In that split second of waiting, he wondered if this was what it was like to die.

The rider jerked backward in the saddle and slid off the back. He fell to the ground with a terrible thud.

It was then that Ned realized that the shot had come from behind him. Lina had fired it. Ned reined back and looked down at the man who had fallen right beside him. The gunman's face was gone. There was not enough of it left to even tell that it had once been a human face.

Ned looked over his shoulder as Lina rode up beside him, her pistol still smoking. She took one look at the man she'd killed and looked away.

"You saved my life, Lina," he said softly.

She sighed deeply as she holstered her pistol, and then she rode a few feet away from the grotesque scene. Killbuck and the two deputies rode back and joined Ned and the girl.

The gunfight had lasted only three minutes. Three men were dead and another was so badly wounded, he would have to seek a doctor.

None of them spoke of the gunfight as they rode back toward the Red River Station building.

"Let's check the cattle in the stockyard," Ned said.

Lina and the men followed him over to the stockyard where hundreds of cattle mingled. The stench was awful and the bawling of the animals was almost unbearable. Ned and the others dismounted and tied their horses to the pole fence.

"I guess I'd better ask permission to examine the cattle," Ned said. He walked around to the office and while he was gone, Lina and the others walked through the unlocked gate and wandered among the cattle, checking the brands.

By the time Ned came back, Lina had found what they were looking for. "Here it is," she called to him.

Ned examined the brand carefully and saw that it had been altered with a running iron so that it now looked like a double diamond, instead of a mirrored M. A line now connected the center of the letter M to the center of the letter W.

Ned walked back to the office and asked the thin,

balding stockyard keeper if he could purchase one of the cattle.

"Just one?" the keeper grumped.

Ned noticed the man's name on a plaque on the paper-littered desk.

"Yes, Mr. Jones. Just one," he said. "I want you to come look at it and tell me whose brand it is."

The nearly bald man looked at Remington's badge and then glared at Ned. Nevertheless, he stood up and followed Ned back to where the others were waiting. In the meantime, the deputies had rounded up ten more cattle with the same brand.

"Whose brand is this?" Ned asked politely as he pointed to the brand.

"It's the Double-Diamond brand," Jones said sullenly.

"I can see that, Mr. Jones. Who does it belong to?" Ned demanded.

Again, the stockyard keeper gave Remington a dirty look. He hesitated before he finally answered. "That's one of Van Hook's brands."

"How many brands does he have?" Ned asked.

"I don't know. I don't keep track of such things," Jones said. "Ain't none of my business."

"You know these are rustled cattle, don't you?" Ned asked.

"I wouldn't know about that," Jones replied.

"You'd better know about it," Remington said. "I could arrest you right now for receiving stolen goods."

"I didn't receive nothin'," Jones said. "I don't own no cattle. This is a public stockyard, Marshal. Ranchers from all over this territory pay me to keep their cattle until they can either sell them or herd them to market."

"You sell these cattle, don't you?"

"Sometimes, if a buyer happens along."

"Do you know what the penalty is for selling stolen property, Mr. Jones?"

"I got nothin' to do with where these damned animals come from. If I happen to sell some of them, I take a percentage of the sale, which has been agreed upon by me and the ranchers beforehand. I run an honest business here, Marshal. I don't own a damned single one of them cattle and I couldn't tell you whether they were stolen or not. Like I say, it ain't none of my business."

"Where does Van Hook live?" Ned asked.

"I wouldn't know."

"Yes, you do. I'll arrest you for selling stolen cattle if you don't want to cooperate."

"You threatening me, Marshal?"

"Just stating a fact. In Judge Barnstall's court, the penalty's pretty stiff for having stolen goods in your possession."

"I told you they ain't my cattle," Jones said. "Van Hook lives west of here, near Nocona."

"That's what I was told," Ned said.

"If you already know where he lives, then why in the hell're you askin' me?" Jones snarled.

"Just seeing how honest you are. How much do you want for this bull?"

"Twenty-five dollars," Jones said.

"Shouldn't be more than five dollars on the hoof," Ned objected.

"Van Hook sets the price for his cattle, not me."

"It's a big bull," Ned said. "I'll give you six dollars, no more."

"Go ahead and take it," Jones said. "Just leave me alone so I can get back to my paperwork."

"Don't I get a bill of sale?"

"For six lousy bucks, you don't need it," Jones grumbled as he stalked away.

"That's because you don't want a record of the sale, Jones," Ned called after him. "That money's gonna go right in your pocket and Van Hook'll never know about it."

Jones ignored the remark and slammed his office door when he went inside.

Ned tied a rope around the bull's neck and led it out of the stockyard. "Frank, will you come with me?" he asked.

"Yes," Frank said without question.

"Tom, take Lina and Charlie to the cafe around the corner and buy them some breakfast. We'll meet you there in a little while."

After Tom and the others left, Ned and Frank mounted their horses and Ned led the bull by the rope to a field just beyond the stockyard. Ned climbed down from the saddle, drew his pistol and shot the bull between the eyes. The animal's legs went wobbly under his weight and then it toppled over on his side. Frank shot him again in the heart, just to make sure he was dead.

Ned dug a sharp, thin, sheathed knife out of his saddlebags, and a small jar of salt. Ned cut around the brand, leaving an inch of hide around the outside of the circle. He slid the sharp knife under the circle and sliced it away from the flesh. Frank watched over his shoulder as Ned turned the piece of hide over and scraped all of the flesh away from the inside of the hide.

"No doubt about it," Frank said. "That was the Mirror M brand."

"Yes," said Ned. "The M and W are very clear. They're old scars, deep scars. The added line doesn't even show on the inside of the flesh."

"Looks like Van Hook's men just ran these cattle through the chute and jabbed them with the running iron."

Ned scraped the inside perfectly clean, then salted it. "I'll take this back to Barnstall for evidence," he said as he tucked it into his pocket.

"What now?" Frank asked.

"Now we get the others and head to Van Hook's ranch near Nocona. He won't be expecting us because he thinks we're already dead."

"What about the gunman who got away?" Frank asked.

"He won't get out of town. He's lost too much blood by now."

Chapter Fourteen

Remington and his group spent the rest of the day in the saddle, except when they stopped to rest their horses and when they stopped for a quick snack. They stopped for the night just before they got to Nocona and slept out under the stars. Ned didn't want to ride into the town after dark.

They arrived in the small town the following morning about nine o'clock. Nocona proved to be a town that was very hostile toward the U.S. marshals. It seemed like Peter Van Hook was a big man in this small pond. And when they talked to the local sheriff, Lafe Parsons, they discovered that Parson's was in the rancher's pocket, too.

At three o'clock in the afternoon, when Remington realized he wasn't going to get any information about the location of Van Hook's ranch, he decided to try the Shawnee Saloon. Surely there would be someone in there who could be bought for a cheap drink. Since he didn't want Lina out of his sight, he took her with them. She was dressed like a man and nobody would notice her anyway.

Ned wasn't surprised to find the saloon crowded that time of day. That was the kind of town Nocona was. Drunks and no-accounts all over the place. After checking the gloomy, smoke-filled room to see if Gaton and Haskins were there, he found an empty table in a corner, near the front. He pulled up an extra chair and after Killbuck, Lina and Frank Shaw were seated, Ned and Tom Beck strolled over to the long bar.

"What'll you have?" the barkeep asked.

"A pitcher of beer and five glasses," Ned said. He knew Lina wouldn't drink, but it wouldn't look right if she didn't have her own glass. He took a dollar out of his pocket and slid it across the counter.

"We don't serve Indians in here, Marshal," the homely barkeep said. "It looks like you'll only be needing three glasses."

"Make it three, then," Ned said.

The barkeep picked up the dollar. "If you'll ask your two friends to leave, I'll be happy to serve you, sir."

"We've come a long way, my friend," Ned said as he pulled another dollar from his pocket and set it on the counter. "My two friends just want to rest a spell. If you'll let them stay, we'll have just one quick drink and then be gone."

"One short drink," the barkeep said as he picked the second dollar up with his thumb and forefinger. He turned and took three smudgy glasses off a shelf, dipped each in a keg beneath the shelf and slid the three half-full glasses across the counter.

"Thank you," Ned said. "Can you tell me where I can find Peter Van Hook's ranch?"

"Two dollars ain't gonna buy you that kind of information," the barkeep said smugly.

"How much will it take?" Beck asked.

"I don't rightly know where he lives, so keep your money."

Ned knew the man was lying in his teeth, and he also knew that it wouldn't do any good to push it.

"Thanks anyway," he said. He picked up two of the glasses and left the third one for Tom to carry back to the table. Without sitting down, Ned took a small sip out of his glass, then set it on the table. He walked over to another table where two obviously-drunk men were sitting. "Pardon me, sir, can you tell me where Peter Van Hook lives?" he asked politely of the older man.

"He ain't gonna tell you, so leave him alone," the younger man said in a slurred voice.

"Why don't you let him speak for himself," Ned said.

" 'Cause he's too drunk."

"His ranch is hidden in the woods," said the older man.

"Shut up, Curt," said the other.

"Where abouts in the woods," Ned persisted.

"A mile down the road, and a half a mile to the right," the older man slurred before his friend could shut him up.

"Shut up, Curt," his companion said again as he clenched his fist.

"My friend here works for him. Danny can show you the way."

"You fool," Danny shouted to the older drunk.

"Thanks, Mister," Ned said politely. He turned away.

"I told you to leave him alone," shouted the younger drunk. He shoved his chair back and it tipped over in a loud crash.

Ned glanced around just in time to be punched in the mouth. He wiped the corner of his mouth and glared at his attacker. He had the information he needed and he wanted to get out of there.

Beck wasn't seated yet and he stepped over to make sure Ned was all right. Killbuck jumped up just as the man named Danny struck out at Beck. Tom stuck his arm up to ward off the blow and a fellow at a nearby table leaped up and slugged Beck a good chop under the chin. Killbuck picked up a glass of beer and threw the contents in the man's face.

Within a minute a slug-fest broke out in the whole saloon and customers were hitting each other for no reason other than to fight.

Lina jumped up from her seat and tried to get out of the way. Danny took another swing at Remington. Ned ducked and Danny hit Lina's hat instead.

Lina screamed just as her hat fell off. Her long hair tumbled down past her shoulders.

"He's a girl!" a rough-looking drunk shouted as the fighting continued.

Danny, the lad who worked for Van Hook, stepped up to Lina and ripped the front of her shirt, popping all of her buttons. Her bare breasts were exposed and she quickly drew the torn blouse back around her. The fighting got wilder, with chairs being broken across heads. Lina used the opportunity to grab her hat and ease toward the batwing doors. She stopped, faced the wall, and tucked her hair back under her hat, then quickly held her blouse together again.

Danny started after her, but Ned punched him in the stomach and when the drunken lad doubled over, Ned brought his fist up hard into the fellow's chin.

Danny stumbled backwards, tripped over a broken chair and crashed to the floor.

"Let's go," Ned whispered to the others. He grabbed up Lina's hand and dragged her outside. Nobody seemed to notice that Remington and his friends were leaving. They were all too busy fighting.

"Well, you got the information you needed," said Beck when they were outside, "but that's the hard way to get it." He rubbed a sore chin.

"I'm sorry, Lina, if you were embarrassed," Ned said.

"I'm just glad no one was hurt," she said.

Ned glanced at the batwing doors of the noisy saloon. "Let's get away from here before Danny picks himself up off the floor and comes after us."

Although Ned was tempted to run, the group of five walked down the street at a normal pace so they wouldn't draw attention. They went to the livery, a block away and around the corner, where they had paid a friendly old man three dollars to watch their horses and their belongings.

"You depities come back at just the right time," the old man said with a toothless grin. He sat in a hard rocking chair near the door. His loaded rifle was propped against the wall near him. "My wife just done called me for supper."

"Well, good." Ned was relieved when he glanced at the horses and saw that all of their rifles and saddlebags were still in their places. "Thanks for taking such good care of our animals."

"I watered 'em and grained 'em, just like I promised to."

"Thank you," said Tom Beck.

"I still say three dollars is more'n I'm worth."

"You earned it, Gramps," said Shaw.

"I wantcha all to know that if you hadn't came back just now, I would'a stayed right here," the fellow assured them.

"I know you would have, oldtimer," Ned smiled.

"I'da made Sophie bring my supper right on out here," the fellow chuckled. "I ain't so old but what I can eat and watch horses at the same time."

Ned laughed. "Well, you'd better toddle off before your supper gets cold."

"You sure you won't be needin' me no more?"

"Not right now," Ned said. "We just came for our horses."

The oldtimer's knees creaked when he stood up. "You young pups be careful," he said as he hobbled toward the door. "Like I told ya, this town's full of wicked people. Used'ta be a feller felt safe in his own home. Not anymore. I don't know what's happening to this new generation," he said as he went on out the door.

Ned could hear Gramps mumbling to himself right up to the time the old man went into his own house and closed the door. "What a character." Ned shook his head and walked over to his horse.

"Gramps couldn't have done much to protect our gear if it came to that," Shaw said.

"No, but he was the only friendly face in town."

Lina opened her saddlebag and took out the wrinkled dark brown shirt she'd been wearing when they started out from Tishomingo two days ago.

"If you gentlemen will turn your backs, I'll change my shirt before we leave," she said.

The four men walked over to the open door.

"Are we going out to Van Hook's now?" Beck asked.

"Yes," Ned said. "And I hope Gaton and Haskins are out there, too, so we can round them all up and get the hell out of here."

"I'm through," Lina called.

The men went back to their horses. Ned walked on over to the girl.

"Lina, we're going to Van Hook's ranch, but I don't want you to go."

"Why not?" she said.

"Too many people know you're a girl and if Van Hook finds out, it won't take him any time at all to figure out who you are. We can't risk it now."

"But how would he find out?"

"It wouldn't surprise me any if that fellow Danny beat us out there. And Van Hook owns most of the people in town. Somebody'll tell him."

Charlie Killbuck walked over and stood next to his niece.

"I guess you're right," Lina said.

"Yes, he is," Killbuck said.

"Do you want me to wait for you here?" Lina asked Ned.

"No. Charlie, I want you to take Lina over to the Nocona Hotel while my deputies and I ride out to arrest Van Horn. Don't leave her alone for a minute."

"I will watch over her," Charlie promised. "I will get a room on the second floor, if I can. It will be safer."

"Maybe you should leave your horses here and take only your weapons," Ned suggested.

"Yes," said Killbuck. "We can walk along behind the buildings and no one will see us."

"Good."

Lina stood up on tiptoes and kissed Ned on the cheek. "Be careful, Ned," she said.

For a brief moment, Ned thought about Katy and how she used to stand on her tiptoes to kiss his cheek. She always used to laugh and tell him he was too tall. And the sickening feeling came to his stomach when he remembered that it had been three long years since she'd kissed him that way.

"You, too, Lina," he said. "You be careful."

Ned mounted his horse. Already he could feel the knot of tension at the back of his head. He had no idea what he and his men would be facing when they got to Van Hook's ranch, but he knew it wouldn't be pleasant. A feeling of apprehension and uncertainty settled over him as he rode out of the stable.

Shaw and Beck were right behind him and he checked his surroundings, as he always did. He rode the few feet to the main street of town and looked both ways. He turned south.

"I hope we're going in the right direction," he said.

"The fellow at the saloon said a mile down the road and a half a mile to the right," Tom Beck said.

"I know. 'Down the road' means south to me. I wonder if it means the same thing to him."

"There's only one way to find out," Shaw said. "If we're wrong, we come back and start again."

Ned chuckled, but he didn't feel the least bit jovial. Inside, it felt like furry caterpillars were crawling all over his nerves. He wasn't afraid of danger. It was just the not knowing.

"Well, gentlemen," he said, "this may be the showdown we've been waiting for."

Chapter Fifteen

Ned Remington had no trouble at all following the drunk's directions. He and his men rode south on the road from Nocona, about a mile, he figured, until they came to a side road. They turned right and it wasn't long until they saw the woods. The path that had been cleared through the woods was narrow and the deputies rode single file.

"Are you going to just ride right in there and arrest Van Hook?" Frank Shaw asked.

"That's what we're here for," Ned answered. "I see no need to sneak up on him. He knows we're coming."

When the three deputies emerged from the woods, a vast expanse of land stretched out in front of them. A huge ranch house sat in the middle of the estate, some fifty yards away, and Ned spotted the four men in the front yard right away.

As Remington had expected, Van Hook's henchmen were waiting for them. The fellows looked like cowhands and Ned was surprised that there were only four of them. He had expected more. Still, Van Hook would not be easy to take. He didn't see Van Hook and figured he was inside the house.

Ned didn't stop, nor did he ride in fast. He kept his horse at a slow, even pace as he rode toward the house. Behind him, Shaw and Beck now rode two abreast, flanking him. Sitting tall and straight on their mounts, they looked like a small army marching proudly to war.

As they rode forward, Remington took in as much as he could with his eyes. The large, elegant ranch house sprawled all over the place. It was two stories high and looked out of place in this desolate part of the country. It was a house that belonged in the fanciest section of a big city. Remington had no doubts that the ranch house had been paid for by Van Hook's illegal schemes.

Ned scanned the dozens of windows at the front of the house, searching for some sign of Peter Van Hook. The curtains at every window were drawn tight.

The grass seemed to go on forever. It was tall and lush, much like the grass in the pastures of the Cherokee village in Tishomingo. There were a few trees in the yard, but no flowers or shrubs or walkways to make the place pretty. It was obvious that Peter Van Hook had no interest in esthetics. He was more interested in what money could buy him.

There were several outbuildings and way off to the left, were hundreds of heads of cattle, confined by a pole fence. The smell of their droppings was strong in the air. Remington wondered if some of those cattle belonged to Woody Miller. He wished he could check them out, but he had the evidence he needed in his pocket. Regardless, he was sure that all of the cattle had been rustled.

The four cowhands who had been standing together near the porch when Ned had first seen them, had now wandered out into the yard. They stood a few feet apart, hands hovering over holstered pistols.

Ned held the reins loosely in his left hand. His other hand rested on his upper thigh, near his own holstered pistol.

Nobody spoke. The two groups of opposing men just stared at each other and waited for the other to make the first move.

Remington could feel the tension build as he and his men rode closer to the ranch house, closer to the cowhands who were waiting to kill them. He expected them to start shooting at any minute and wondered why they hadn't already.

The front door opened and Peter Van Hook stepped out on the porch. Remington knew it was Van Hook from Mike Madonna's description. Neatly dressed in fancy clothes, a business suit and polished boots, nice enough looking, the fringes of neat blond hair that stuck out beneath the white hat. Ned wasn't quite close enough to see the rancher's blue eyes, but he knew they would be cold and hard and vacant, like Madonna had said.

"Are you Peter Van Hook?" Remington asked in a loud voice.

"Yes I am," Van Hook answered in an equally loud voice.

"I'm Ned Remington, United States Chief Deputy Marshal," Ned said. "I have a warrant for your arrest, Mr. Van Hook."

"For what?" Van Hook answered.

"For receiving stolen goods," Remington called.

"Open fire, men," Van Hook told his cowhands. "Shoot to kill."

The marshals fanned out as the cowhands snatched their pistols out of smooth holsters.

Ned whipped out his pistol and fired at the bewhiskered cowhand who was aiming at him. He shot low, just a brief instant before the other man fired. Ned's bullet slammed into the cowhand's kneecap.

The anticipation of getting hit was enough to throw the cowhand's aim off at the last minute. His shot was high and the bullet zinged over Ned's head. The cowhand screamed out in pain. He dropped to the ground and clutched his leg.

Remington swung on another man as Frank Shaw fired a round. Frank's shot was right on the mark. The tall cowhand he fired at staggered backwards then crumpled to the ground, his heart exploded.

Two more shots were fired almost simultaneously and their echoes reverberated through the air.

Ned squeezed the trigger and dropped the barrel-chested cowhand who had run up behind Frank's horse and was just about to fire at the back of Frank's head. Ned's shot crashed through the man's leg and shattered bone.

Tom Beck had missed his first shot. The second one plowed straight through the heart of the only cowhand still standing. The man would die soon, but not as quickly as the one Shaw had killed.

Suddenly the fight was over, with two of the cowhands dead, the other two badly wounded. The acrid stench of gunpowder would last a lot longer.

Ned turned his horse toward the porch and trained his pistol on Van Hook. The rancher eased his hand toward his holster.

"Don't even think about it, Van Hook, or you'll

have three bullets in your head instead of just one," Ned warned him.

Frank and Tom rode up from behind and positioned themselves on either side of Remington, their weapons aimed at the wealthy rancher.

"You're under arrest, Van Hook," Ned repeated. "I have the warrant right here in my pocket." He tapped his hide jacket.

Ned eased down from his saddle and got a pair of handcuffs out of his saddlebags. He walked toward the porch, his pistol still aimed at the rancher.

Shaw and Beck dismounted and followed Ned to the porch.

"You'll never get me to court," Van Hook bragged as the three deputies walked up the steps. "I've got too many friends."

"When you get through in Judge Barnstall's courtroom, you'll wish we had killed you on the spot," Remington told him.

Ned holstered his own weapon, then reached over and slid Van Hook's pistol out of its holster. He tucked it into his belt. With Frank Shaw's help, Ned handcuffed Van Hook's hands behind his back. Shaw patted the rancher down to make sure he didn't have any concealed weapons.

"Where are Paco Gaton and Norville Haskins?" Remington demanded.

"I don't know," Van Hook said.

"We'll find them," Remington said.

"I'm sure you will," Van Hook said sarcastically.

It was then that Ned saw how dark and cold and vacant Van Hook's blue eyes were.

After they got Van Hook's horse from the stable, the three deputies and their prisoner rode back to Nocona. It was late in the afternoon and the sun would be gone in another half hour. As they neared the Nocona Hotel, Ned wondered which room Killbuck and Lina were staying in. He glanced up the windows.

Too late, Remington saw the movement on the roof of the hotel. A shot rang out and an instant later, Frank Shaw gasped, then moaned in agony.

"Dammit," Ned said as he glanced over at his friend. He drew his pistol and aimed it up at the roof. Beck drew, too, but kept his eyes on their prisoner in case he tried to escape during the commotion. Ned scanned the roof line, but there was no one up there, at least not that he could see.

"Where'd you take the bullet?" he asked Shaw as he rode around to Frank's side. He saw the stain of crimson spread across Frank's upper sleeve.

"In the arm," Frank said as he clutched his arm beneath the wound and held it close to his body in an attempt to stem the bleeding.

"How bad is it?"

"I don't know," Shaw said. "It feels numb right now."

"Let's get you inside the hotel where we can take a look," Ned said. He looked up at the roofline again. Something caught his attention. Movement at one of the windows.

Ned was shocked when he saw the two men who had suddenly appeared in one of the upstairs windows. One of the men was Charlie Killbuck. The other man was a Mexican and Ned knew right away that it was Paco Gaton. Paco had a gun to Charlie's head.

"They got Charlie," he said as he drew his pistol. He wondered if Lina was up there, too.

Beck had noticed the movement, too, and was already looking up at the window, his pistol in hand.

"Then the fellow on the roof must be Haskins," Beck said.

"Release Van Hook and I'll let your friend go," Paco shouted from the open window.

"We can't do that, Gaton," Remington called back. "You let Charlie go. I've got a warrant for your arrest."

"I ain't interested," Paco shouted. "You let Van Hook go or I'll shoot your friend in the head."

A crowd began to gather on the street, but they kept their distance. Ned didn't like it. Peter Van Hook had too many friends in this damned town.

Remington wished he could get a clean shot at the Mexican, but he couldn't risk hitting Charlie. "We won't let Van Hook go, Gaton," he shouted. "We're taking him in."

A shot cracked the air.

Remington watched with horror. He was sick when he realized that Paco had actually shot Charlie Killbuck in the temple.

"The dirty sonofabitch!" Tom Beck said.

"My God," Frank Shaw muttered. "Poor Charlie." He still held his arm tightly.

"You bastard!" Ned shouted.

Charlie slumped forward onto the windowsill, the side of his head blown away. Paco shoved the body on out the window. The Cherokee's body fell two stories and slammed to the hard ground with a loud thunk. The body landed ten feet away from Ned.

Both Beck and Remington fired at the window, but Paco ducked out of sight.

"Tom, I'm going up there," Ned said. "I think

Lina's up there." He started to dismount.

"Too late," Beck said as he stared up at the open window.

Ned glanced up and saw Lina in the window with Gaton. The Mexican shoved the pistol against her temple.

"Let Van Hook go," Paco demanded. "Release him right now or your lady friend will end up the same way her poor uncle did."

"The bastard," Remington mumbled. He couldn't let Lina down the way he had Charlie. "All right, Gaton," he called up. "We'll let Van Hook go if you release Lina."

"Then do it now," Paco shouted.

"Let the girl go," Remington demanded. He and Beck dismounted so they could untie their prisoner.

"After Van Hook is free," Paco said.

Ned and Tom quickly unfastened the thongs that bound the rancher. "We'll get you later, Van Hook," Ned said. "You're going to be punished for your part in this cattle rustling operation."

Peter Van Hook didn't answer. He just took the reins in his hands and rode away.

"Van Hook is free," Remington called. "Let Lina go now." He glanced up at the window and saw that Lina and Paco Gaton were not there. "Dammit, I'm going up there and get Lina," he told Beck. "Can you get Frank inside the hotel?"

"Yes, but you be damned careful, Ned. Paco might be waiting for you."

"I will." Remington ran inside the hotel and dashed up the stairs. He figured out which room Lina would be in and didn't bother to knock when he got there. He tried the door handle and found it wasn't locked. With his pistol drawn, he shoved the door wide open and then hesitated as he peered into the room.

He didn't hear any sounds from within the room, but he knew it was the right one. Straight ahead of him was the open window and the blood-stained windowsill.

His breath caught in his throat as he cautiously stepped into the small room and looked in both directions. He checked under the bed and even looked behind the straight-back chair.

Lina Miller wasn't there and neither was Paco Gaton.

"That dirty bastard," Ned said out loud.

Chapter Sixteen

Remington dashed back downstairs and saw Frank and Tom sitting in the lobby. Tom was checking Frank's gunshot wound.

"Lina's not up there," Ned said in an excited voice. "Paco's gone, too. He's kidnapped her."

"We'll find them, Ned," Tom said.

"How bad is the wound?" Remington asked.

"Not too bad," Tom said. "The bullet went clean through the flesh. The desk clerk said there was a doctor up the street and I'm going to take Frank up there."

"Go ahead," Ned said. "I'm going to check out back. I'll meet you at the doctor's office in a few minutes."

Ned stopped at the counter and asked the desk clerk if he had seen Lina and the Mexican come downstairs.

"No," the clerk said, "but I haven't been here all the time. After the shooting, I went to fetch the sheriff. I just got back."

"Thanks anyway," Ned said. He dashed down the hall and went out the back door. It was already dark outside. He didn't see anybody in the alley. He walked around but couldn't find anything that indicated that Lina and the Mexican had been there. He didn't have a lantern and it was too dark to see much. In the starlight he did notice that there were a lot of hoof prints in the loose dirt, but he figured those belonged to customers of the hotel.

Frustrated, he walked back through the hotel lobby, and then went to the doctor's office. The elderly doctor gave Ned the report that he had cauterized the wound and wrapped it in sterile bandages. The doctor gave Ned a bundle of sterile clothes and told him to change the dressings at least once a day. He informed him that there was a chance that the wound would still become infected.

Ned paid the doctor for his services and after the three deputies left the doctor's office, Ned informed them that they had to track the girl down.

"I think the outlaws teamed up and took Lina with them," he said as he and Tom helped Frank up in his saddle.

"Van Hook, too?" Tom asked. "Do you think he's with them?"

"I think so. And I don't think they'll kill Lina as long as they think we're tracking them. Paco knows that I won't risk her life. As long as they've got her, they'll figure we won't get too close."

"You're probably right, Ned."

"You're the tracker in the family, Tom. You got any idea where they might have gone?"

Tom shook his head. "Hell, they could be anyplace. They could have gone back to Van Hook's ranch. That would have been the smartest thing to do, but since we know where it is, they probably won't risk it. We don't know where Paco and Haskins live, do we?"

"No," said Ned. "But since the cattle rustling operation seems to center around here and the Red River Station, Van Hook has probably provided them with a hideout shack somewhere between here and there."

"Didn't someone tell us that Paco and Haskins were staying at a little town near the Red, downstream from Tishomingo?" Beck asked.

"Yes. You think they went there?"

"Hell, for all we know they could be out on another raid." Tom said. "And that could be anywhere from here to the Nations, or on over to Arkansas, or maybe even Missouri. It ain't gonna be easy."

"What about you, Frank?" Ned asked. "Do you feel up to riding tonight?"

"Not really," Frank said, his voice weak.

"Tonight?" Beck said. "There's not much we can do tonight except to ride around in circles and check out our hunches. It'd be better to wait until morning when I can look for tracks."

"I figure they're going to be riding all night to put some miles between us," Ned said. "If so, they may get too far ahead of us for us to ever find them."

"That's a chance we'll have to take, Ned. They've got to stop sometime to sleep. And Van Hook's a prissy old lady. He ain't gonna want to be sleeping on the hard ground. Not when his money can buy the best hotels and food in the country."

"We'll wait until morning, then," Ned agreed. "Maybe you'll be feeling better by then, Frank."

* * *

In the morning, Frank Shaw was stronger. He felt good except for the throbbing pain in his arm.

The three deputies left the Nocono Hotel at dawn and rode south far enough for Beck to know that he hadn't found the tracks he was looking for. They turned around, rode back through town, and checked the tracks again when they were out on the open road.

Tom finally found what he was looking for. One set of hoof prints was shallow and it was made by an unshod horse. That would be Lina's Indian pony. He had noted before that her pony was unshod. He found a distinguishing mark on another set of hoof prints. One of the horseshoes had a triangular-shaped nick in it.

"They're headed for the Red River," he told the others.

For the next two days, the deputies took almost the same path they had covered before as they tracked the outlaws north to Tishomingo. And then for the next four days they backtracked on the same well-traveled road they had used to get to Tishomingo, losing sight of the tracks at times, picking them up again further along the trail. Not once in all that time did they see Lina or the outlaws, but Tom assured them that they were making progress and that the foursome was still riding together.

It wasn't until they reached Sallisaw, near the Arkansas border, that things changed.

"Lina's not riding with them anymore," Beck said after examining the tracks for several miles after he first discovered that the unshod pony's tracks were not with the others.

Remington became alarmed. "What does that mean?" he asked. "Do you think they killed her?"

"Maybe not," Beck said. "Maybe she escaped from them."

Chapter Seventeen

The deputies backtracked to the place where Tom had first discovered that Lina's tracks were missing. After walking in all different directions, carefully examining the ground, he finally found Lina's tracks again.

"Lina's alive," Tom said.

"Thank God," Ned sighed.

"She escaped from her captors. The tracks seem to be headed for Tahlequah."

"I think she's heading home to Osage," Remington said. "My guess is that she'll go through Siloam Springs."

"I think you're right about her heading home," Shaw said. "But Tahlequah would be out of her way." His arm was healing nicely and hardly hurt anymore.

"She probably went that way to throw the outlaws off guard if they tried to follow her," Beck said.

"She's smart enough to do it," Ned said.

"Now we've got a big decision to make," Tom said. "Do we follow Lina, or do we follow the outlaws?"

"There's no question about it," Remington said.

"We go after Lina. Once we find her, we can always go after the outlaws."

"Then do we to to Tahlequah or Siloam Springs?" Beck asked.

"Siloam Springs," Ned said. "I know she'll be there and it'll cut out a lot of time. If we're closing in on them as fast as you say we are, Tom, we might even beat her there."

"We will beat her there, if my calculations are right," Beck said.

The men headed for Siloam Springs and got there early in the morning of the third day.

Siloam Springs was quiet when they arrived. The deputies took up a position in a grove of trees where they could watch the road from Tahlequah.

They waited and waited. The hours dragged by and the men were sure they had made a wrong decision. They were about to leave when they saw a lone rider heading toward them.

Twenty minutes later, Lina Miller rode up, totally exhausted. Her horse was lathered, almost ready to cash it in.

"They're right behind me," she cried. Ned helped her down from her saddle and she fell into his arms. "I just knew they were going to catch up to me today," she sobbed. "They're trying to kill me."

"It's all right now, Lina," Ned said as he wrapped his arms around her. "We'll help you."

"I know you will," she sobbed. "I never thought I'd see you again."

"Tom Beck is the best tracker around. He knew at every turn in the road just where you were going. He

told us that you escaped from the outlaws near Sallisaw."

Lina pulled away from Ned. "That's amazing," she
said.

"Tom also told us you were going to Tahlequah,"
Ned said.

"I did," she laughed. "I didn't want them to know
I was going back to Arkansas so I went the long way
around."

Ned Remington looked off in the distance and saw
the spools of dust kicked up by the fast-approaching
horses. "They're coming fast," he said.

Lina and the two deputies turned and saw the
riders.

"Give me a rifle or your spare pistol," Lina said to
Ned.

"You're in no condition to fight, Lina," he said.
"Just stay out of sight and let us handle it. Besides, I
want these men alive."

"Why?" she asked. "Haven't they killed enough?"

"They're going to trial," Ned said. "I want them to
stand trial in front of Judge Barnstall."

"All right," she said. "I won't shoot to kill. But,
let me help. Please."

Reluctantly, Ned gave her an extra pistol and the
ammunition to go with it. They all tucked back into
the grove of trees.

As the riders came on fast, Ned kicked Lina's
horse and sent it out onto the trail. The trick worked.
The outlaws charged.

"Shoot low," Ned said. "Try to hit the horses, not
the men."

He took aim and shot Paco Gaton's horse in the
leg. The horse faltered and went down. Gaton

slammed to the ground and the horse rolled over on his legs.

Lina shot Peter Van Hook's horse right out from under him.

Norville Haskins whirled his horse around and made a break for it just as Remington took aim. Ned adjusted his aim and shot at the retreating horse. His shot was high and he hit the rider instead. Haskins tumbled from his saddle, a bullet in his back.

Van Hook was up and running and Tom Beck chased him down, tackled him to the ground. Beck dragged him back over to the trees and Frank Shaw helped him put the handcuffs on.

Paco Gaton cursed a blue streak as he struggled to free himself from the weight of his downed horse. Ned and Beck walked over and pulled the animal's legs off of the outlaw. They shackled him on the spot.

Haskins was still alive and not badly wounded. The bullet passed through the fleshy ring of fat just below his ribs. He crawled into the thick brush while the others were busy with the other outlaws.

A few minutes later, Remington heard the click of a cocking pistol. He turned around just in time to see Lina running toward the brush. He knew the clicking sound had come from the brush. He glanced around and didn't see Haskins on the ground where he had fallen from his horse. And then he knew. Haskins was in the brush, prepared to kill one of them.

"No, Lina!" he called just as the girl disappeared into the brush.

A shot rang out and Ned was certain that Lina had been killed.

Ned and Tom approached the brush cautiously. The brush rattled and they jumped back just as Lina emerged from the thick brush, carrying the pistol.

"I—I only had one bullet left," she said in a shaky voice.

"What about Haskins?" Remington asked.

"He's in there. Dead."

"Did you have to kill him?"

"Yes. He was going to kill one of you. I fought off his advances when I was with them. He hurt me very badly. He has been trying to kill me all along. I hated him. That's what finally gave me the courage to escape from those dreadful murderers. I wanted to kill all of them. I still do."

"You'd better give me that pistol," Ned said.

She looked over at the two prisoners with hatred in her eyes. "Yes, maybe I should," she said bitterly.

She handed the Colt to Ned.

Ned let out a sigh of relief. He spun the cylinder around and saw that there was still one shot left. He looked at Lina.

"That was for me, if I missed," she said softly.

Remington looked hard at her for a long time. A muscle twitched in his jaw.

"Let's go," he said gruffly. "Tom, mount 'em up."

"Sure," said Tom. He glanced at Lina and shook his head. "I'm sure glad she's going to come willin'," he told Ned.

"So am I, Tom," Ned said with a smile. "So am I."